HFD
D0337253
Get more out of libraries
Please return or renew this item by the last date shown.
You can renew online at www.hants.gov.uk/library
Or by phoning 0300 555 1387
Hampshire
County Council
CHRISTMAS
Stories
WITHDRAWN
C016125794

MICHAEL MORPURGO
CHRISTMAS Stories

EGMONT

Contents

In memory of so many wonderful Christmases together:
For Edna, Mac, Seonaid and Stuart,
and for all their families since.

M.M.

THE GOOSE IS GETTING FAT

Illustrated by Sophie Allsopp

Gertrude was a goose like any other goose. Hatched out in the orchard one drizzly morning in June, she spent those early weeks looking at the world from the warm sanctuary of her mother's all-enveloping softness. It might have come as a surprise to her to know that her mother was not a goose.

Of course Gertrude was convinced she was, and that was all that mattered; but in reality her mother was a rather ragged speckled hen. She was, however, the most pugnacious, the most jealous and possessive hen on the farm, and that was why Charlie's father had shut her up inside a coop with a vast goose egg and kept her there until something happened. Each day she had been lifted off and the egg sprinkled with water to soften the shell. The summer had been dry that year, and all the early clutches of goose eggs had failed. This was very probably the last chance they had of rearing a goose for Christmas.

There had always been a goose for Christmas Day, Charlie's father said – a goose reared on their own corn and in their own orchard. So he had picked out the nastiest, broodiest hen in the yard to guard the egg and to rear his Christmas goose, and Charlie had sprinkled the egg each day.

When Charlie and his father first spied the golden gosling scavenging in the long grass with the speckled black hen clucking close by, they raced each other up the lane to break the good news to Charlie's mother.

She pretended to be as happy about it all as they were, but in her heart of hearts she had been hoping that there would be no goose to rear and pluck that year. The job she detested most was fattening the goose for Christmas and then plucking it. The plucking took her hours, and the feathers flew everywhere, clouds of them – in her hair, down her neck. Her wrists and fingers ached with the work of it. But worst of all, she could not bear to look at the sweet, sad face she had come to know so well, hanging down over her knee, still smiling. She would willingly pluck a pheasant, a hen, even a woodcock; she would skin and gut a rabbit – anything but another goose.

Now Charlie's father was no fool and he knew his wife well enough to sense her disappointment. It was to soften the news, to console her and no doubt to persuade her again, that he suggested that Charlie might help this year. He had his arm round Charlie's shoulder, and that always made Charlie feel like a man.

"Charlie's almost ten now, lovely," he said. Charlie's father always called his mother 'lovely', and Charlie liked that. "Ten years old next January, and he'll be as tall as you next Christmas. He'll be taller than me before he's through growing. Just look at him, he's grown an inch since breakfast."

"I know Charlie's nearly ten, dear," she said. "I was there when he was born, remember?"

"Course you were, my lovely," Charlie's father said,

taking the drying-up cloth from her and sitting down at the kitchen table. "I've got a plan, see. I know you've never been keen on rearing the goose for Christmas, and Charlie and me have been thinking about it, haven't we, Charlie?"

Charlie hadn't a clue what his father was talking about, but he grinned and nodded anyway because it seemed the best thing to do.

"We thought that this year all three of us could look after the goose, you know, together like. Charlie boy can feed her up each day and drive her in each night. He can fatten her up for us. I'll kill her when the time comes – I know it seems a terrible thing to do, but what's got to be done has got to be done – and perhaps you wouldn't mind doing the little bit of plucking at the end for us. How would that be, my lovely?"

Charlie was flattered by the confidence his father had placed in him and his mother was, as usual, beguiled by both his Welsh tongue and the warmth of his smile. And so it was that Charlie came to rear the Christmas goose.

The fluffy, flippered gosling was soon exploring every part of the orchard and soon outgrew her bad-tempered foster mother. The hen shadowed her for as long as she could. Then she gave up and went back to the farmyard.

The gosling turned into a goose, long and lovely and white. Charlie watched her grow. He would feed her twice a day, before and after school, with a little mixed corn. On fine autumn days he would sit with her in the orchard for hours at a time and watch her grazing under the trees. And he loved to watch her preening herself, her eyes closed in ecstasy as she curved her long neck and delved into the white feathers on her chest.

Charlie called the goose 'Gertrude' because she reminded him of his tall, lean Aunty Gertrude who always wore feathers in her hat in church. His aunt's nose was so imperial in shape and size that her neck seemed permanently stretched with the effort of seeing over it. But she was, for all that, immensely elegant and poised, so there could be no other name for the goose but Gertrude.

And Gertrude moved through her orchard kingdom with an air of haughty indifference and an easy elegance that sets a goose apart from all other fowl. To Charlie, however, Gertrude had more than this. She had the gentle charm and sweetness of nature that Charlie warmed to as the autumn months passed.

They harvested cider apples in late October, so Gertrude's peace was disturbed each day for over two weeks as they climbed the lichen-coated apple trees and shook until the apples rained down on the grass. Gertrude and Charlie stood side by side waiting for the storm to pass, and then Charlie moved in to gather up the apples and fill the sacks. Gertrude stood back like a foreman and cackled encouragement from a distance. Her wings were fully grown now, and in her excitement she would raise

herself to her full height,
open her great white wings,
stretch her neck, and beat the
air with wild enthusiasm.

"It's clapping, she is," said
Charlie's father from
high up in the tree.
"A grand bird. She's
growing well. Be fine by
Christmas if you look after
her. We've got plenty of
Bramley apples this year,
good for stuffing. Nothing like
apple stuffing in a Christmas
goose, is there, Charlie?"

The words fell like stones on Charlie's heart. As a farmer's son he knew that most of the animals on the farm went for slaughter. It was an accepted fact of life; neither a cause for sorrow nor rejoicing. Sick lambs, rescued piglets, ill suckling calves – Charlie helped to care for all of them and had already developed that degree of detachment that a farmer needs unless he is to be on the phone to the vet five times a day. But none of these animals were killed on the farm – they went away to be killed, and so he did not have to think about it. Charlie had seen his father shoot rats and pigeons and squirrels but that again was different, they were pests.

Now, for the first time, as he watched Gertrude patrolling behind the dung heap, he realised that she had only two months to live, that she would be killed, hung up, plucked, pulled, stuffed and cooked, and borne in triumph onto the table on Christmas Day. "Nothing like apple stuffing in a Christmas goose" his father's words would not go away.

Gertrude lowered her head and hissed at an intruding gaggle of hens that flew up in a panic and scattered into the hedgerow. She raised her wings again and beat them in a dazzling display before resuming her dignified patrol. She was magnificent, Charlie thought, a queen among geese. At that moment he decided that Gertrude was not going to be killed for Christmas. He would simply not allow it to happen.

With the frosts and winds of November, the last of the leaves were blown from the trees and swirled round the farmyard. Then the winter rains came and piled them into soggy, mushy heaps against the hedgerows, clogging the ditches and filling the pot-holes. It was fine weather for a goose, though, and Gertrude revelled in the wildness of the winter winds. She stalked serenely through the leaves, her head held high against the wind and the rain, her feathers blown and ruffled.

Each day when Charlie got back from school he drove Gertrude in from the orchard to the safety of an empty calf pen. Foxes do come out on windy nights, and he did not want Gertrude taken by the fox any more than he wanted her carved up at Christmas. Before breakfast every morning Charlie opened the calf pen, and the two of them walked side by side out into the orchard where he emptied the scoop of corn into Gertrude's bowl. He talked to her all the while of the great master-plan he had dreamed up and how she must learn not to cackle too loudly.

"Won't be long now, Gerty," he said. "But if you make too much noise, you're done for. Your goose will be cooked, and that's for sure." But Gerty wasn't listening. She had found a leafy puddle and was busy drinking from it, dipping and lifting her head, dipping and lifting . . .

Until late November his father had not taken much interest in Gertrude's progress, but now with Christmas only six weeks away he was asking almost daily whether or not Gertrude would be fat enough in time.

"She'll do better on oats, Charlie," he said onc breakfast. "And I think you ought to shut her up now, and I don't mean just at night. I mean all the time. This wandering about in the orchard is all very well, but she won't put on much weight that way. There won't be much left on her for us, will there? You leave her in the calf pen from now on and feed her up."

"She wouldn't like that," Charlie said. "You know she wouldn't. She likes her freedom. She'd pine away inside and lose weight." Charlie had his reasons for wanting to keep Gertrude out in the orchard by day.

"Charlie's right, dear," his mother said softly. "Of course you're both right, really." His mother was the perfect diplomat. "Gertrude will fatten up better inside, but it's lean meat we want, not fat. The more natural food she eats and the happier she is, the better she'll taste. My father used to say, 'A happy goose is a tender goose'. And anyway, there's only the three of us on Christmas Day, and Aunt Gertrude, of course. What would we do with a fifteen-pound goose?"

"All right, my lovely," said Charlie's father. "I know better than to argue when you and Charlie get together. But feed her on oats, Charlie, else there'll be nothing on her but skin and bone. And remember I have to kill her about a week before Christmas – a goose needs a few days to hang. And then you'll need a day or so for plucking and

dressing, won't you, lovely? I can smell it already," he said, closing his eyes and sniffing the air. "Goose and apple stuffing, roast potatoes, sprouts and chipolata sausages. Oh Christmas is coming and the goose is getting fat!"

The days rolled by into December, and Christmas beckoned. There was a Nativity play at school in which Charlie played Joseph. There were the endless shopping expeditions into town when Charlie dragged along behind his mother, who would never make up her mind about anything. Christmas with all its heady excitement meant little to Charlie that year for all he could think of was Gertrude. Again and again he went over the rescue plan in his mind until he was sure he had left nothing to chance.

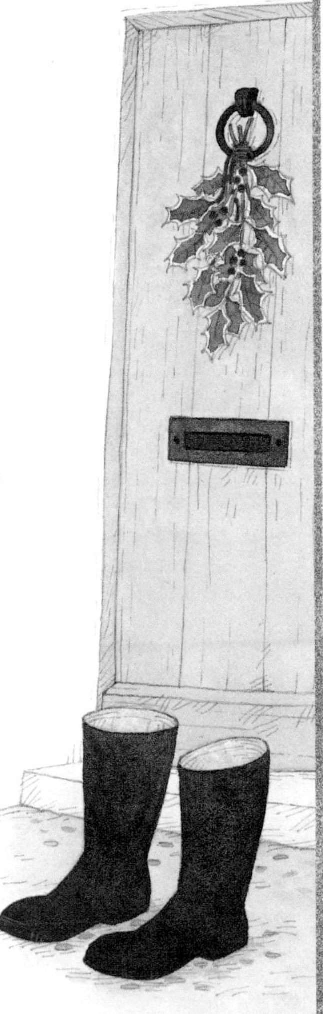

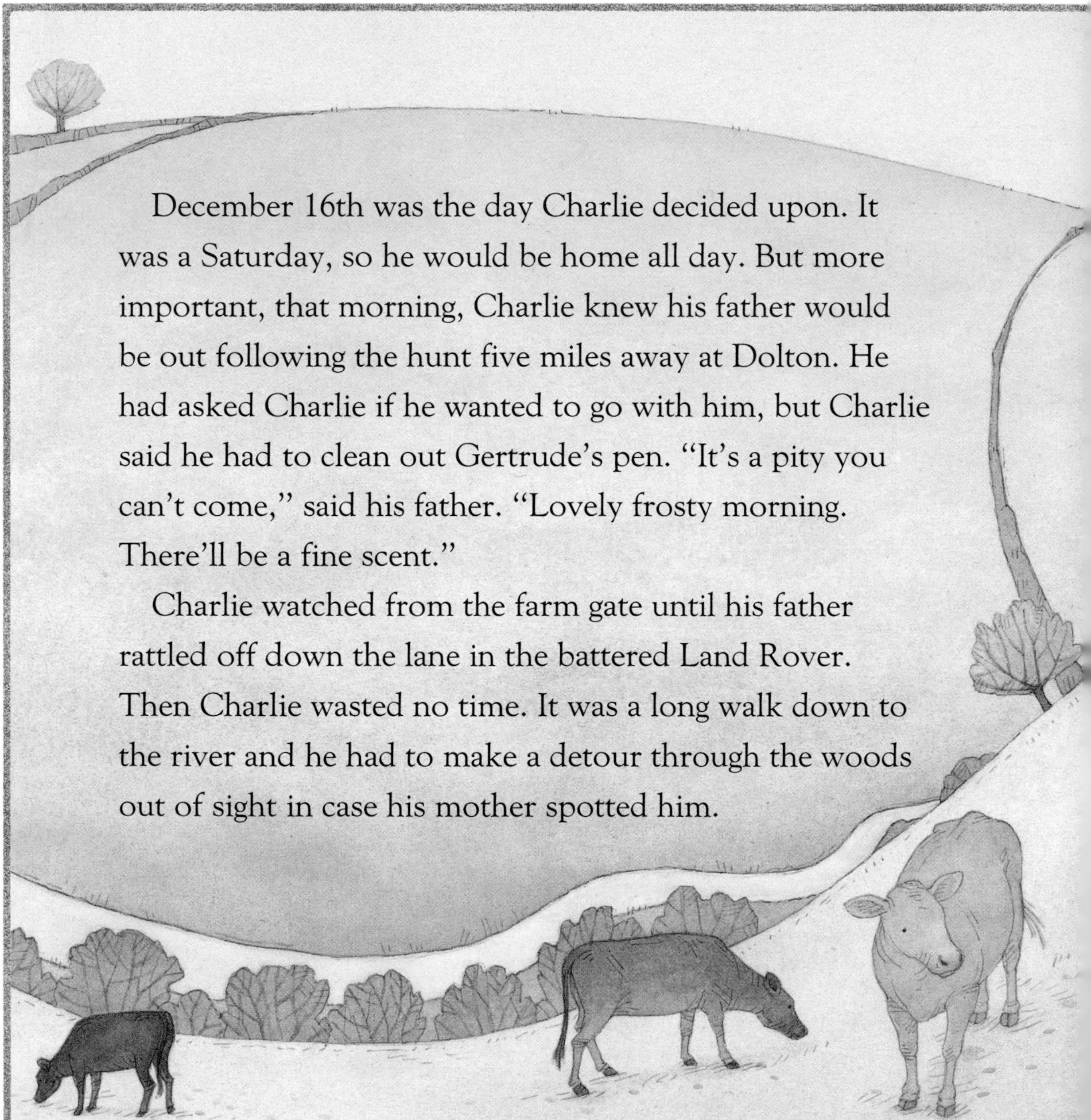

December 16th was the day Charlie decided upon. It was a Saturday, so he would be home all day. But more important, that morning, Charlie knew his father would be out following the hunt five miles away at Dolton. He had asked Charlie if he wanted to go with him, but Charlie said he had to clean out Gertrude's pen. "It's a pity you can't come," said his father. "Lovely frosty morning. There'll be a fine scent."

Charlie watched from the farm gate until his father rattled off down the lane in the battered Land Rover. Then Charlie wasted no time. It was a long walk down to the river and he had to make a detour through the woods out of sight in case his mother spotted him.

Gertrude was waiting by the door of the calf pen as usual, impatient to get out into the orchard. But this morning she was not allowed to stop by her bowl of corn. Instead she was driven firmly out into the field beyond the orchard. She protested noisily, cackling and hissing, trying to get back by turning this way and that. But Charlie paid no attention. He banged his stick on the ground to keep her moving on. "It's for your own good, Gerty, you'll see," he said. "It has to be far away to be safe. It's a hiding place no one will ever find. No one goes there in the winter, Gerty. You'll be as safe as houses down there, and no one will eat you for Christmas. Next year you'll be too tough to eat anyway. They say a goose can live for forty years.

Think of that – not six months but forty years. So stop making a fuss, and walk on."

He talked to her all the way down through Watercress Field, into Little Wood and out into Lower Down. By the time they reached the marsh, Gertrude was exhausted and had stopped her cackling. Every gateway was a trial, with the puddles iced over. Try as she did, the goose could not keep her balance. She slithered and slipped across the ice until she found the ground rough and hard under her feet again. All the while the stick beat the ground behind her so that she could not turn around and go home.

The fishing hut stood only a few yards from the river, an ugly building, squat and corrugated, but ideal for housing a refugee goose.

In the last few days Charlie had moved out all the fishing tackle. He had laid a thick carpet of straw on the floor so that Gertrude would be warm and comfortable. In one corner was the old hip bath he had found in the attic. The bath was brim full of water and Charlie had hitched a ramp over the side. By the door was a feeding trough already full of corn. But Gertrude was not impressed by her new home. She walked straight to the darkest end of the hut and hissed angrily at Charlie. He rattled the trough to show her where the corn was, but the goose looked away disdainfully. Her whole routine had been rudely disturbed and all she wanted to do was to sulk.

"You'll be all right, Gerty," said Charlie. "But if you do hear anyone, don't start cackling. You've got food and water, and I'll be down to see you when I can. I can't come

too often. It's a long way and they might get suspicious."
Gertrude hissed at him once again and turned her head away. "I love you too!" said Charlie, and he went out, bolting the door firmly behind him.

Charlie ran back all the way home because he needed to be breathless when he got there. His mother was just finishing icing the cake when Charlie came bursting in through the kitchen door. "She's gone. Gertrude's gone. She's not in the orchard. She's not anywhere."

Charlie and his mother searched all that morning and through the afternoon until the frost came down with the darkness and forced them to stop. Of course they found no sign of Gertrude.

"I can't understand it," said Charlie's mother, as they broke the news to his father. "She's just vanished. There's no feathers and no blood."

"Well I can't believe it's a fox, anyway," said Charlie's father. "Not in broad daylight with a hunt just on the other side of the parish. She's in a hedge somewhere, laying an egg perhaps. They do that in winter sometimes, you know. She'll be back as soon as she gets hungry. It's a pity, though. She'll lose weight out in the cold."

Charlie's mother was upset. "We'll never find her if it snows. They've forecast snow tonight."

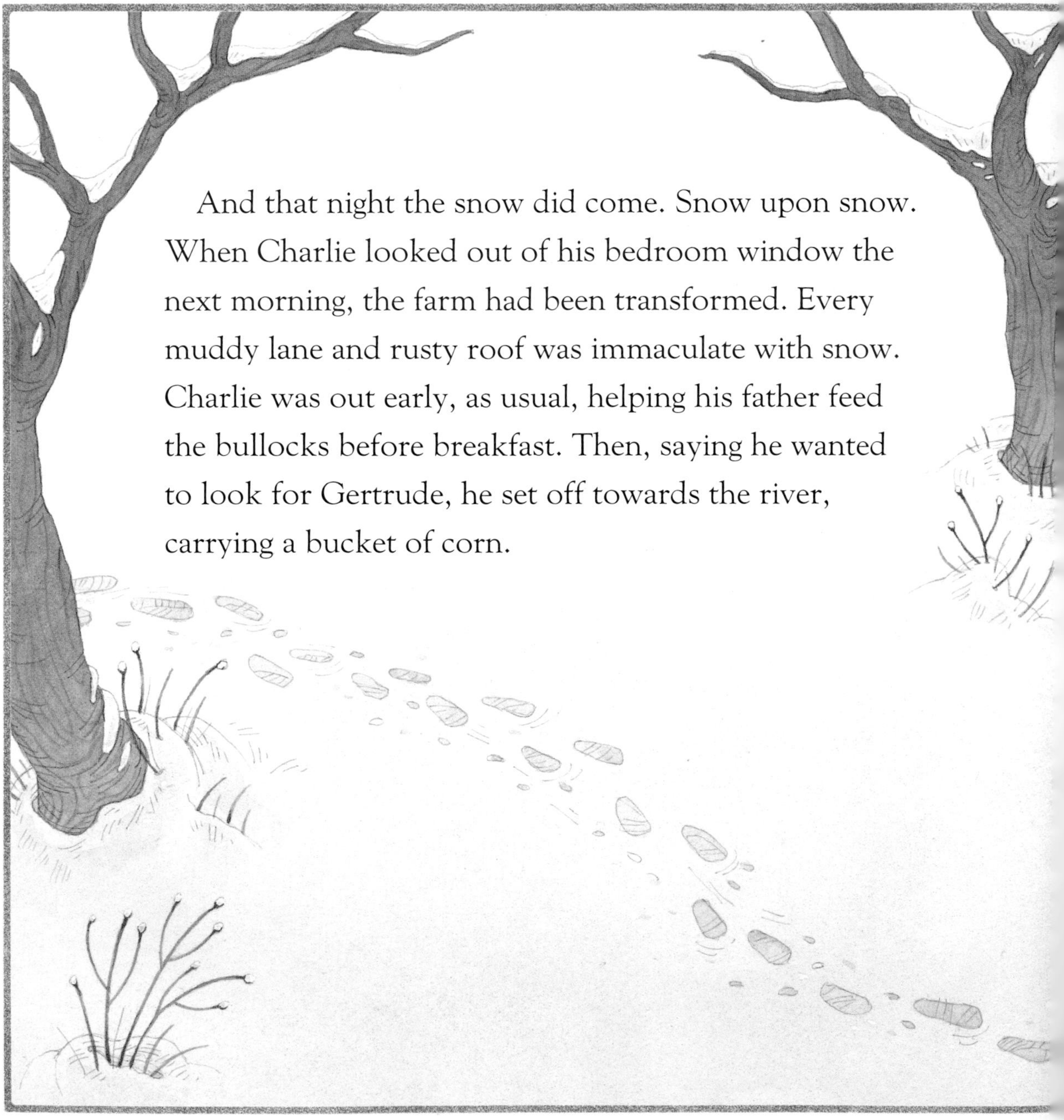

And that night the snow did come. Snow upon snow. When Charlie looked out of his bedroom window the next morning, the farm had been transformed. Every muddy lane and rusty roof was immaculate with snow. Charlie was out early, as usual, helping his father feed the bullocks before breakfast. Then, saying he wanted to look for Gertrude, he set off towards the river, carrying a bucket of corn.

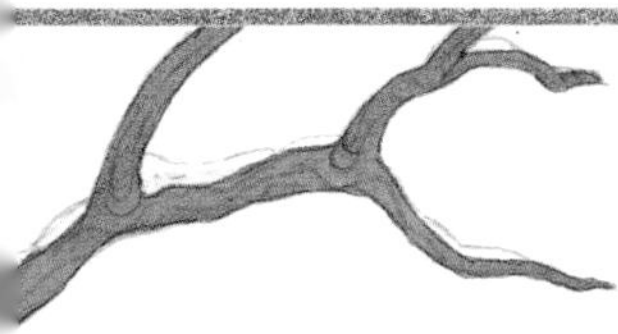

Gertrude hissed as he opened the door of the fishing hut, but when she saw who it was, she broke into an excited cackle and opened her wings in pure delight. She loved Charlie again. Charlie poured out the corn and topped up the water in the hip bath. "So far, so good, Gerty," he said. "Not so bad in here, is it? Better in here than out. There's snow outside, but you'll be warm enough in here. Father thinks you're laying an egg in a hedge somewhere. Mother's worried sick about you. I can't tell her until after Christmas, though, 'cos she'd have to tell Father. But she'll understand, and she'll make Father understand, too. See you tomorrow, Gerty."

Every day for a week, Charlie trudged down through the snow to feed Gertrude. By this time both his mother and father had given up all hope of ever finding their Christmas goose. "It must have been a fox," his mother reflected sadly. "Gerty wouldn't just have walked off. But you'd think there would have been a tell-tale feather or two, wouldn't you? Don't be upset, Charlie."

Charlie had always found it easy to bring tears to his eyes and he did so now. "But she was my goose," he sniffed. "It was all my fault. I should have shut her up like Father said."

"Come on, Charlie," said his father, putting an arm round him. "We can't have all these tears over a goose, now can we? After all we were going to eat her, and have you ever heard of anyone crying over Christmas dinner?"

Charlie was proud of his tearful performance, but was careful not to overdo it. "I'll be all right," he said manfully. "I'm going to keep looking, though, just in case."

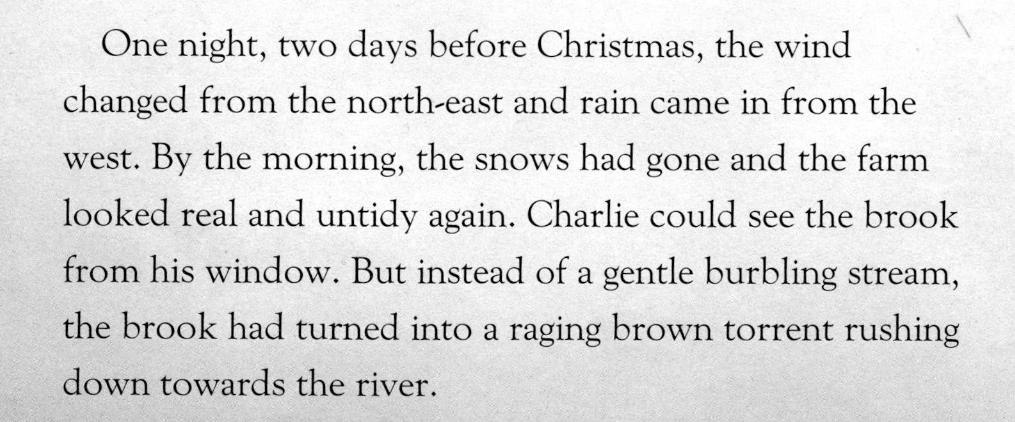

One night, two days before Christmas, the wind changed from the north-east and rain came in from the west. By the morning, the snows had gone and the farm looked real and untidy again. Charlie could see the brook from his window. But instead of a gentle burbling stream, the brook had turned into a raging brown torrent rushing down towards the river.

The river! If the river burst its bank the fishing hut would be under water, and Gertrude would be trapped inside. She wasn't used to swimming. Her feathers would be waterlogged and she would drown.

He dressed quickly and within minutes was running down towards the river. As he opened the gate into the marsh, he could see that the hut was completely surrounded by water and that the door was wide open.

He splashed through the floods, praying that he would find Gertrude still alive and safe. But Gertrude wasn't even there. The trough and the straw floated in a foot of muddy water, but of Gertrude there was neither sound nor sight.

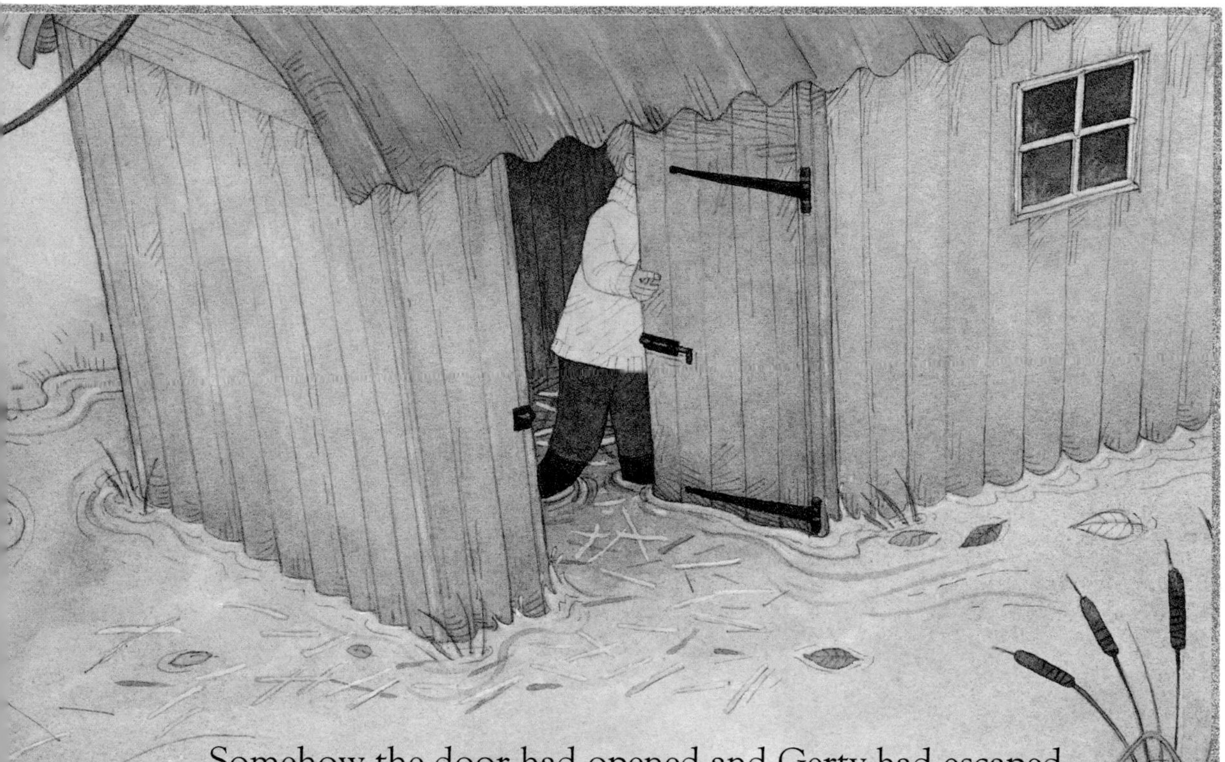

Somehow the door had opened and Gerty had escaped. He must have forgotten to bolt it, and the force of the flood water had done the rest. Now Gertrude was out there somewhere in the floods on her own. This time she had really escaped and when Charlie cried he really meant it, and the tears flowed uncontrollably.

Charlie spent the rest of the day searching the banks of the river for Gertrude, calling everywhere for her. But it was no use. The river was still high and flowing fast. He could only think that she had been swept away in the floods and drowned. He was filled with a sense of hopeless despair and wretchedness. He longed to tell his mother, but of course he could not.
He dared not even show his feelings.

In the evening Aunty Gertrude arrived, for it was Christmas Eve. A tree was brought in and together they decorated it before joining the carol singers in the village. But Charlie's heart was not in any of it. He went to bed and fell asleep without even putting his stocking out.

But when he awoke on Christmas morning the first thing he noticed was his stocking standing stiff as a sentry by his bedside table. Intrigued and suddenly excited, he felt to see what was inside the stocking. All he found was a tangerine and a piece of long, stiff card. He pulled out the card and looked at it. On it was written:

To Charlie, from Father Christmas:
Goosey Goosey Gander, where shall I wander?
From the orchard to the fishing hut,
From the fishing hut to the hay-barn . . .

It was clearly his
mother's handwriting.

Charlie tiptoed downstairs
in his dressing gown, 
slipped on his wellingtons and
then ran out across the back yard
to the hay-barn.

He unlatched the little wooden door
and stepped inside. In the farthest
corner, penned up against a wall of hay
were two tall geese that cackled and hissed at his approach.

They sidled away together into the hay, their heads almost touching. Charlie crept closer. One was a splendid grey goose he had never seen before. But the other looked distinctly familiar. And when she stretched out her white wings, there could be no doubt that this was Gertrude.

But his attention was drawn to a beautifully decorated card, which read:

To Dearest Charlie from Gertrude,

I've got a message from your mother and father.

Your mother says you should remember that if you walk in snow you leave footprints that can be followed.

And your father says: Nice try, Charlie boy.

We're having chicken for lunch today.

Aunty Gertrude likes it better, anyway. Look after the geese. You'd better. They're yours for keeps!

So Charlie, meet Berty – he's a gander. He's my husband, Charlie, a present from Father Christmas, and I hope you like him as much as I do. Oh, and by the way, thanks for saving my neck. I couldn't have asked for a better friend.

Much love for Christmas,

By the time Charlie got back to the house, everyone was sitting down in the kitchen and having breakfast. Aunty Gertrude wished him a Happy Christmas and asked him what he'd had in his stocking. "A goose, Aunty," he said, smiling. "And a tangerine!"

Charlie looked at his mother and then at his father. Both were trying hard not to laugh.

"Happy Christmas, Charlie boy, any sign of Gertrude yet?" his father asked.

"Yes," said Charlie, swallowing his excitement. "Father Christmas found her and brought her back – and Berty too – her husband, you know. Nice of him, wasn't it?"

"Gertrude?" said Aunt Gertrude, looking bewildered. "A goose in your stocking?" She looked over her nose just like a certain goose. "I don't understand. What's all this about?"

"Later, dear," said Charlie's mother, gently patting her sister's arm. "I'll tell you about it later, after we've eaten our Christmas dinner!"

To Basil and Adrian,
Puppeteers Supreme!

M.M.

THE BEST OF TIMES

Illustrated by Emma Chichester Clark

There are times when all seems well with the world. It was just such a time when this story begins. Everyone in the whole country was happy. The harvest was looking good. The corn grew gold in the fields. The vines and the trees were heavy with fruit. The shining rivers teemed with silver fish.

But happiest of all in this lucky land was Prince Frederico. He was more like a brother than a prince to his people, and much loved, which was why everyone was so happy for him when he found at last the Princess of his heart, Princess Serafina. She was a girl of such beauty and kindness that everyone who saw her took her to their heart at once. She only had

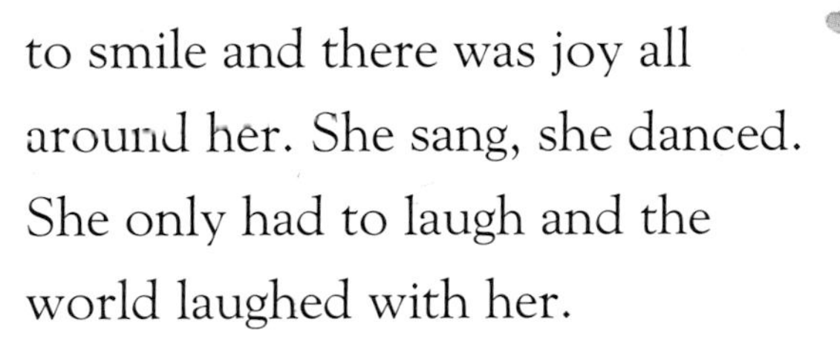

to smile and there was joy all around her. She sang, she danced. She only had to laugh and the world laughed with her.

The two married on New Year's Day, and the people went mad with joy. They rang the bells all over the land. They danced in the streets, they rousted and revelled, they feasted and fêted, from morning till night. Never had anyone seen such a happy couple.

But a year or so later, all this had changed. The joy and the gladness had gone. Everyone could see that a great sorrow was settling over the Princess, like a dark shadow.

She never smiled any more, nor laughed any more. She did not sing. She did not dance. She did not speak for days on end. Sometimes she would not even eat. Prince Frederico simply could not understand what had come over his beloved Princess, nor could anyone else. It was a complete mystery.

The light left her eyes. The glow left her cheeks. Every evening, the Princess would sit beside her Prince in the great hall of the palace, not touching her food, speaking to no one. She seemed lost in her own sadness, and could find no way out.

Prince Frederico was desperate to make her happy again. He did all he could to cheer her heart.

At Christmas time, as a token of his love for her, he lavished gifts upon her. Dresses of the finest silk. Rubies and emeralds and sapphires he gave her too, and a pair of white doves that cooed to her from her window when she woke in the mornings. He gave her parakeets and peacocks, meercats and monkeys, and two whippets to stay always by her side and love her faithfully.

But nothing seemed to raise her spirits. No husband could have been more kind and loving than the Prince. He tried his very best to find out why it was, how it was, that she had become so wrapped up in her sorrows.

"We can be happy together again, dearest," he told her. "All will be well, I promise. If only you would just tell me what it is that is troubling you so, then I could help to make things right for you, and make you happy again. Is it something I have done?"

But the Prince's kind words, like all his wonderful gifts, simply left her cold. She turned her head away and kept her silence. Even when he held her in his arms and kissed her fondly, she still seemed far away from him and lost in her sadness. The Prince was heartbroken. There seemed to be nothing whatever he could do to

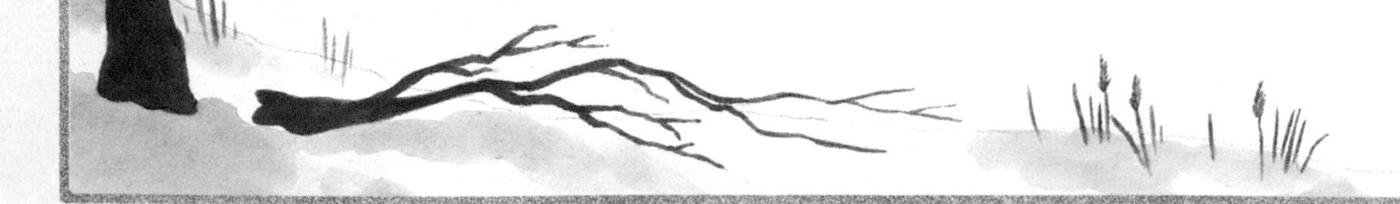

help her. The royal physician visited her every day, but he was as baffled and mystified as everyone else. No medicine he gave her made any difference.

For poor Princess Serafina there was no escape from her sorrows, even in her dreams. All night long she would lie awake. All day long she would sit in her room, ignoring all the food Prince Frederico brought to her, however sweet it smelt, however spicy. A little fruit was all she would eat, and a little water to drink. That was all. She was overwhelmed by sorrow. Maybe after the grey skies of Winter had passed, the Prince thought, maybe then she would be happier.

Spring came at long last, and there was birdsong again, and daffodils danced in the sunshine. But the Princess remained as sad as ever. Prince Frederico was now becoming worried for her life, as was the royal physician.

"She is pining away, my Prince," the physician told him, his eyes full of tears. "She seems to have lost the will to live. If she does not want to live, then there is little I can do, little anyone can do. All I can suggest is that she should get out into the fresh Spring air. Maybe she should go for a ride each day. That might help."

So, the next morning, Prince Frederico took her for a long ride up in the hills, where the air was bright and bracing, where they could look out over the land and see how green and lovely it was under a cloudless blue sky. He put his arm around her.

"Isn't this the most beautiful place on earth, dearest?" he whispered. "It makes you feel good to be alive, doesn't it?"

But Princess Serafina spoke not a word in reply. She gazed out over the cornfields, seeing nothing but emptiness, feeling nothing but loneliness.

By the time Spring turned to Summer, the Princess had become too weak even to ride. The Prince loved her far too much to give up trying. Day after day, he took her out walking in the countryside. But nothing seemed to mean anything to her any more; not the warmth of the breeze on her face, not the buzzards wheeling and mewing over the hillsides, not the lark rising into the sky from the cornfield, not the leaping salmon, nor the whisper of the willows by the river. Nothing touched her heart.

Now it was Autumn. The Princess was too ill by this time to go out any more for her daily walks with the Prince. Instead he sat with her at her window, holding her hand, hoping and praying for the first sign of a miraculous recovery. None came. Gentle morning mists lay over the water-meadows. Trees glowed red and gold and yellow in the afternoon sun. But the Princess saw no beauty in it, took no joy from it at all.

Winter came in with its whining winds and savage storms. The Prince and Princess sat by the fire now in her room, and he would read her stories through the long dark evenings, even though he could tell she wasn't listening. Then, just a week or so before Christmas it was, the Princess became too weak even to rise from her bed. The royal physician shook his head and told the Prince that he knew of nothing that could save her now, that he must prepare himself for the worst.

"No!" cried the Prince. "She will not die. I will not let her die."

But he feared in his heart of hearts that there was nothing more that he could do.

Inside the palace, and outside too, the news quickly spread that the Princess was close to death, that it could only be a matter of time. The Master of the Prince's Household ordered that all preparations for Christmas were to be stopped, that the holly was to be removed, the tree taken down from the great hall, that there would be no Christmas celebrations that year.

All about him, the Prince saw only sympathy and sadness. Friends and family wept openly. It was more than he could bear. He just wanted to get away from it all. He leapt onto his horse and galloped off into the countryside where he could be alone. He rode and he rode, crying out his grief, shouting it into the wind, into the blinding blizzard that was suddenly swirling all around him. On he rode through the snowstorm, not knowing any more how far he had gone, nor where he was, and not caring much either.

Soon his horse could go no further. The snow was too deep, the wind too harsh. So when the Prince saw the light of a cottage window nearby, he knew he had to stop and seek shelter.

But as he came closer and dismounted from his horse, the Prince realised that it wasn't a cottage at all, but a caravan, a travellers' caravan.

He climbed the steps and knocked on the door.

A smiling young lad opened the door and invited him in at once. He did not appear at all surprised to see him. In fact, it seemed to the Prince that this whole family of travellers must somehow have been expecting him, so generous and immediate, so unquestioning was the warmth of their welcome. They saw to the Prince's horse, stabled her with theirs, made sure she had a good rub-down and a feed. Then they sat the Prince down by the stove and gave him a bowl of piping-hot soup to warm him through. In the glow of the lanterns there were a dozen or more faces watching him as he drank down his soup, old and young, but all of them welcoming. There was no sadness here, only smiles and laughter wherever he looked.

None of them seemed to know who he was. He was simply a stranger they had taken in out of the storm.

All evening he stayed with them as they sang their songs and told their stories. Then the old grandfather, the head of the family, leant forward to speak to the Prince.

"You've heard our songs, stranger, and you've heard our stories. Haven't you got a song you'd like to sing for us? Haven't you got a story you'd like to tell?"

The Prince thought for a while. He had only one story on his mind. "It's about a Prince who lived in a palace, and a beautiful

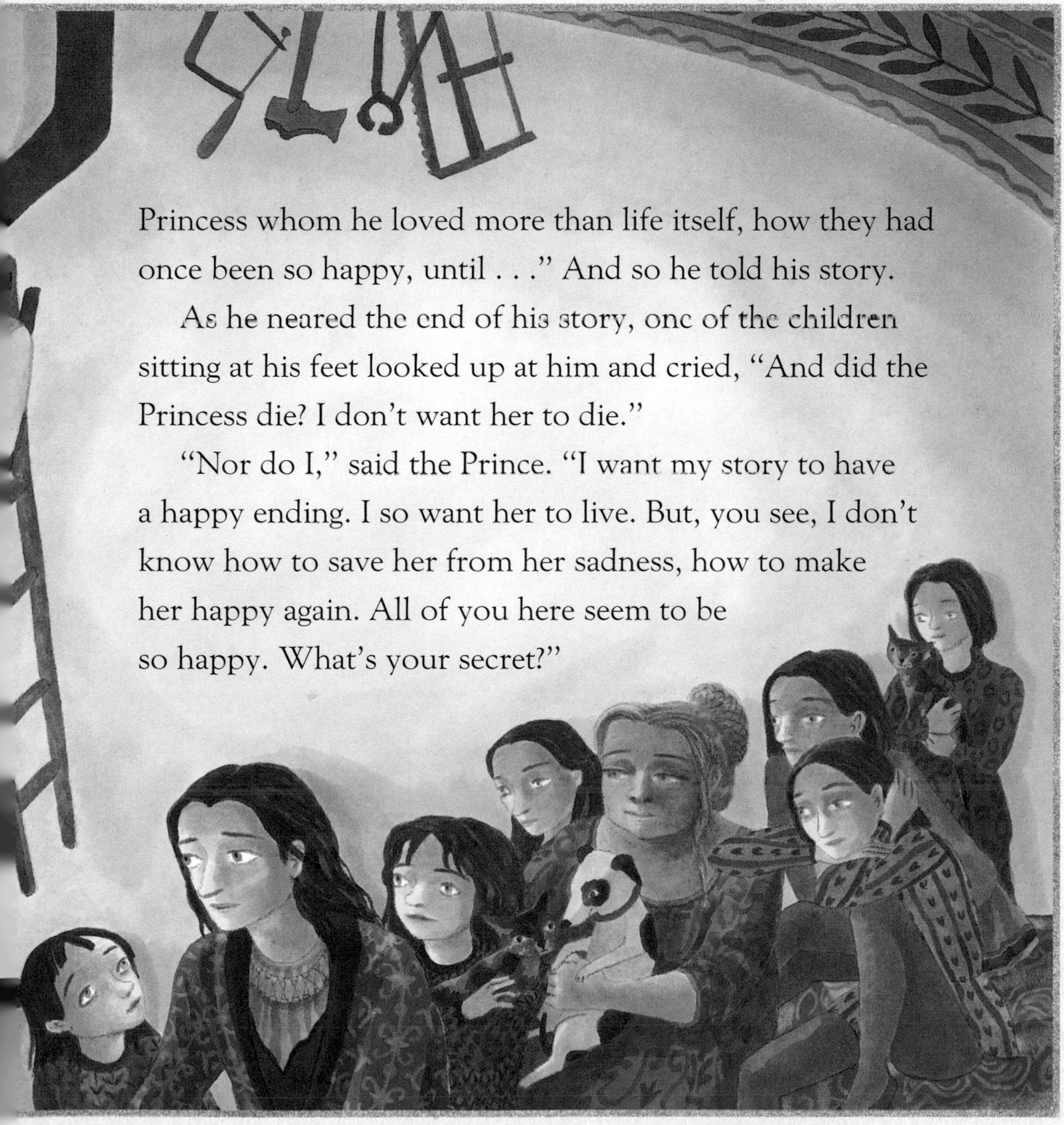

Princess whom he loved more than life itself, how they had once been so happy, until . . ." And so he told his story.

As he neared the end of his story, one of the children sitting at his feet looked up at him and cried, "And did the Princess die? I don't want her to die."

"Nor do I," said the Prince. "I want my story to have a happy ending. I so want her to live. But, you see, I don't know how to save her from her sadness, how to make her happy again. All of you here seem to be so happy. What's your secret?"

"Oh, that's quite simple," replied the old grandfather, knocking out his pipe on the stove. "We are who we want to be. We're travellers, and we keep travelling on. We just follow the bend in the road. Like everyone, we have our troubles, we have our sadnesses. But we try to keep smiling. That's the most important thing of all, to keep smiling. Now, if that Princess in your story could only smile, then she'd be right as rain, and your story would have a happy ending. I like a happy ending. But there's a strange thing about happy endings, they often make you cry, don't they? Funny that. Very close those two, crying and laughing. We need a bit of both, I reckon." The old grandfather lit up his pipe again before he went on. "This Prince of yours, in the story, he loves his Princess very much, doesn't he?"

"More than his whole kingdom," said the Prince. "He'd give his whole kingdom to have her happy again."

"Well then, maybe that's just what he'll have to do," said the old man.

The Prince lay awake all night beside the stove, the travelling family sleeping on the floor around him, and all the while he was thinking of everything the old grandfather had said. Outside, the storm was blowing itself out.

By morning, the Prince had made up his mind what must be done to save his beloved Serafina. He ate a hearty breakfast with the family, and thanked all of them for their kindliness from the bottom of his heart. Then, wishing them a happy Christmas, he set spurs to his horse and rode homeward through the snow, hoping and praying all the way that Princess Serafina would be no worse when he got there.

She was no worse, but she was no better either. Prince Frederico knew there was no time to lose. He called his Council together at once.

"Send out messengers into every corner of this land," he told them. "Tell the people that I will give away my whole kingdom, all my titles, lands and property to anyone who is able to make Princess Serafina smile again."

The Council protested loudly at this, but the Prince

would hear no argument from them.

"I want it proclaimed that whoever can do this, whoever wishes to win my kingdom, must come here to the palace on Christmas Day – and that is only two days away now." He turned to the Master of the Household. "Meanwhile, we shall make merry throughout the palace, throughout the land, as we always do at Christmas time.

I want there to be no more sadness. I want the Princess to feel the joy of Christmas all around her. I want this palace to be loud with laughter. I want to hear the carols ringing out. I want her to smell all the baking pies and puddings, all the roasting pork and geese. I want everything to be just as it should be. We may be sad, but we must make believe we are glad. Let her know that Christmas is the best of times. Let her see it, let her hear it."

And so messengers were sent out far and wide, into every valley, into every hamlet and town in the land.

Meanwhile, as the Prince had commanded, every room and hall in the palace was bedecked again for Christmas, and all the festive fun and games began.

By the first light of dawn on Christmas Day, the courtyard of the palace was filled with all manner of jesters and clowns, jugglers and acrobats and contortionists, all in bright and wonderful costumes, all busy rehearsing their acts. There were animals too – elephants from India, ponies from Spain and chimpanzees from Africa.

Inside the great hall, everyone waited for Prince Frederico to appear and, when at last they saw him coming down the staircase carrying Princess Serafina in his arms, they were on their feet and cheering them to the rafters, willing her to be better, longing for her to smile.

How pale she looked, how frail, so frail that many thought she might not live to see in the new year. But everyone there that Christmas Day knew that this would be her last chance, her only hope, and that they had their part to play. They would do all they could to lift her spirits, to let her know how much she was loved. When at last the great doors opened and in came the first of the performers, a clown with a bucket on his head, they all roared with laughter, all of them glancing from time to time at the Princess, hoping for a flicker of a smile.

One after the other, the clowns and jesters came in to do their turns. They cavorted and capered, they tripped and tumbled, but through it all the Princess sat stony-faced. Jugglers and acrobats, the best in the land, cartwheeled and somersaulted around the hall. They amazed and enthralled everyone there, but not the Princess. Everyone howled with laughter at the contortionists' tangled tricks, but not the Princess.

When the elephants came trumpeting in, the chuckling chimpanzees riding on their backs, when the ponies danced and pranced in time to the music, the Princess looked on bemused, unamused, and empty-hearted. As the last of them left, and the great doors closed after them, a silence fell upon the hall, a silence filled with sorrow. Prince Frederico knew, as everyone did, that it was hopeless now, that nothing on Earth could lighten the darkness for the Princess, that she was lost to them for ever.

But just then, slowly, very slowly, one of the great doors groaned open, and a face peered around. A masked face.

"Who are you?" Prince Frederico asked, as into the hall there came a whole troupe of players. They wore no costumes, only masks. Some were older, some were younger, they could see that. And some were women and some men. But all moved lightly on their feet, like dancers. Together, hands joined, they walked the length of the great hall to where the Prince and Princess sat.

"Who are you?" the Prince asked them once again.

"We are a donkey," said one.

"We are a camel," said another.

"We are a cow."

"We are a sheep."

"We are a goat."

"I am a goose."

"And I am a star," a small voice piped up, holding up high a golden star on a long pole. "And we have all made a puppet play for the Princess, a Christmas play, to please her heart." With that, everyone except the child with the star went out again.

Moments later, a goose appeared at the great door, looking imperiously this way and that, as if the palace belonged to him. And then, bold as brass, as if no one else had any right to be there, he waddled into the great hall, stopping to beckon in after him a sheep and a goat and a cow, life-size all of them, and all of them – the goose too – manipulated by masked puppeteers. They breathed such life into their puppets that, very soon, everyone had eyes only for the animals themselves, and the puppeteers became almost invisible. Organised by this bossy goose, who was fast becoming a favourite with the audience, the animals settled down to sleep under the golden star.

A donkey walked in then, a weary-looking donkey. On his back he was carrying a lady who wore a dark cloak about her – everyone knew it was Mary by now, of course. And leading the donkey was Joseph, who helped her down off the donkey, and led her in amongst the sleeping animals, where he sat her down to rest. They sang a carol together then: "Silent night, holy night, all is calm, all is bright." As they finished singing, Mary opened up her cloak very slowly, and everyone saw there was a baby inside.

A gasp ran around the hall, as everyone saw that the child too was a puppet. His little fists waved in the air. He kicked his legs. He cried out. He gurgled. Suddenly, the Princess was sitting bolt upright, her hand to her mouth, the tears running down her cheeks. Seeing how upset she was, the Prince leapt to his feet at once to stop the play, but before he could do so, she put a hand on his arm.

"Let them go on, dearest," she whispered to him. "I want to see it all, the whole play."

At that moment, in through the great doors there came three camels, masked puppeteers inside them. Living, breathing creatures they were, their heads tossing against their bridles, their tails whisking, chewing and grunting as they came, and each of them ridden by a king bearing gifts.

The goose woke up suddenly, not at all pleased at this unwelcome intrusion. He prowled and hissed around the three kings, head lowered, wings outstretched, as they presented their gifts to Mary and the baby. Then, hissing like a dozen angry snakes, he turned on the camels and chased them off into the night, the three kings running helter-skelter after them. Laughter and clapping filled the hall. The goose took a bow, and then went to have a look at the baby, before settling down again to sleep beside the sheep and the goat and the cow.

Just then, who should come in but several shepherds, looking a bit lost and bewildered. The goose slept on, for the moment. The shepherds found the baby and knelt before him to worship him. Then they sang a carol to him, a lullaby:

"Hush my babe, lie still in slumber,
holy angels guard thy bed,
Sweetest blessings without number,
gently fall upon thy head."

As they sang, the Prince saw the Princess was crying still. Then, like a sudden miracle, she was smiling, smiling through her tears. And by the time the goose woke up, saw the shepherds, and proceeded to chase them, around and around the great hall, she was on her feet and crying again, but with laughter this time.

"I love that goose!" she cried. "I love that goose!"

Everyone was on their feet now, clapping and cheering as the puppeteers came forward to take their bow. The applause went on and on, because everyone could see that the Princess too was clapping and laughing with them, her eyes bright again with life. It was many minutes before the hall had quietened and the Prince could speak.

"You have made my Princess smile," he told the players. "You have made her laugh. So, as I promised, my kingdom is yours."

One by one, players took off their masks, and then the Prince knew them for who they were, that same family of travellers who had sheltered him from the snowstorm, to whom he had told his story.

"We do not want your kingdom," said the old grandfather. "We wanted only to be sure your story had a happy ending, that the Princess could learn to smile again. And now she has. It will soon be the best of times again for her, and for all of you in this happy land."

"Then at least, stay with us a while, stay for our feasting," said the Prince, "so that in some small way I can repay your kindliness and hospitality."

So the players stayed, and feasted, but they would not stay the night. "Travellers," said the old grandfather, as he climbed up into their caravan, "never stay for long. We like to keep travelling on. We just follow the bend in the road. But before we go, we should like to leave you a Christmas gift. Our little goose. We've talked to him about it. He says he's quite happy to live in a palace – just so long as you don't eat him!" And so, leaving the goose behind them, they went on their way into the night. No one knew where they had come from. No one knew where they went. No one ever saw them again.

By Christmas time the next year, Princess Serafina was not only restored to full health and happiness, but she had her own precious baby in her arms, which, of course, was just what the Princess had been longing for all this time. In the play they put on in the great hall that Christmas, the Princess played Mary, and her own child played the baby, kicking his little legs and waving his fists just as he should.

The goose, of course, still insisted on playing the goose. He wasn't the kind of goose you could argue with, everyone knew that. And in his honour – just in case he ever found out – no one in that land ate roast goose at Christmas ever again.

To all those on both sides who took part in the Christmas truce of 1914.

M.M.

THE BEST CHRISTMAS PRESENT IN THE WORLD

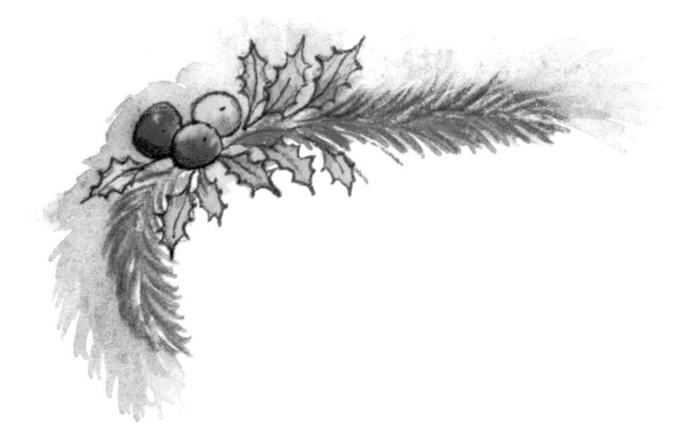

Illustrated by Michael Foreman

I spotted it in a junk shop in Bridport, a roll-top desk. The man said it was early nineteenth century, and oak. I had been looking for a desk like this for years, but never found one I could afford. This one was in bad condition, the roll top in several pieces, one leg clumsily mended, scorch marks all down one side. It was going for very little money, and I reckoned I was just about capable enough to have a go at restoring it.

It would be a risk, a challenge, but here was my chance to have a roll-top desk at last. I paid the man and brought it back to my workroom at the back of the garage. I began work on it on Christmas Eve, mostly because the house was resonating with overexcited relatives and I wanted some peace and quiet.

I removed the roll top completely and pulled out the drawers. Each one of them confirmed that this would be a bigger job than I had first thought. The veneer had lifted almost everywhere – it looked like flood damage. Both fire and water had clearly taken their toll on this desk. The last drawer was stuck fast. I tried all I could to ease it out gently. In the end I used brute force. I struck it sharply with the side of my fist and the drawer flew open to

reveal a shallow space underneath, a secret drawer. There was something in there. I reached in and took out a small blue tin box. Taped to the top of it was a piece of lined note paper, and written on it in shaky handwriting: 'Jim's last letter,
received 25th January 1915.
To be buried with me
when the time comes.'

I knew as I did it that it was wrong of me to open the box, but curiosity got the better of my scruples. It usually does.

Inside the box there was an envelope. The address read: 'Mrs Jim Macpherson, 12 Copper Beeches, Bridport, Dorset'. I took out the letter and unfolded it. It was written in pencil and dated at the top 26th December 1914.

Dearest Connie

I write to you in a much happier frame of mind because something wonderful has just happened that I must tell you about at once. We were all standing to in our trenches yesterday morning, Christmas morning. It was crisp and quiet all about, as beautiful a morning as I've ever seen, as cold and frosty as a Christmas morning should be.

I should like to be able to tell you that we began it. But the truth, I'm ashamed to say, is that Fritz began it. First someone saw a white flag waving from the trenches opposite. Then they were calling out to us from across no-man's-land, "Happy Christmas, Tommy! Happy Christmas!"

When we had got over the surprise

some of us shouted back, "Same to you, Fritz! Same to you!"

I thought that would be that. We all did. But then suddenly one of them was up there in his grey greatcoat and waving a white flag.

"Don't shoot, lads!" someone shouted. And no one did. Then there was another

Fritz up on the parapet, and another.

"Keep your heads down," I told the men. "It's a trick." But it wasn't.

One of the Germans was waving a bottle above his head. "It is Christmas Day, Tommy. We have schnapps. We have sausage. We meet you? Yes?"

By this time there were dozens of them walking towards us across no-man's-land and not a rifle between them.

Little Private Morris was the first up. "Come on, boys. What are we waiting for?"

And then there was no stopping them. I was the officer. I should have called a halt to it there and then, I suppose, but the truth is that it never even ocurred to me. All along their line and ours I could see

men walking slowly towards one another, grey coats, khaki coats meeting in the middle. And I was one of them. I was part of this. In the middle of the war we were making peace.

You cannot imagine, dearest Connie, my feelings as I looked into the eyes of the

Fritz officer who approached me, hand outstretched.

"Hans Wolf," he said, gripping my hand warmly and holding it. "I am from Dusseldorf. I play the cello in the orchestra. Happy Christmas."

"Captain Jim Macpherson," I replied. "And a happy Christmas to you too. I'm a school teacher from Dorset, in the west of England."

"Ah, Dorset," he smiled. "I know this

place. I know it very well."

We shared my rum ration and his excellent sausage. And we talked, Connie, how we talked. He spoke almost perfect English. But it turned out that he had never set foot in Dorset. He had learned all he knew of England from school, and from reading books in English. His favourite writer was Thomas Hardy, his favourite book *Far from the Madding Crowd*. So out there in no-man's-land we

talked of Bathsheba and Gabriel Oak and Sergeant Troy and Dorset. He had a wife and one son, born just six months ago. As I looked about me there were huddles of khaki and grey everywhere, all over no-man's-land, smoking, laughing, talking, drinking, eating. Hans Wolf and I shared what was left of your wonderful Christmas cake, Connie. He thought the marzipan was the best he had ever tasted. I agreed. We agreed about everything, Connie, and he was my enemy. There never was a Christmas party like it, Connie.

Then someone, I don't know who, brought out a football. Greatcoats were dumped in piles to make goal posts, and the next thing we knew it was Tommy against Fritz out in the middle of no-man's-land. Hans Wolf and I looked on and cheered, clapping our hands and stamping our feet,

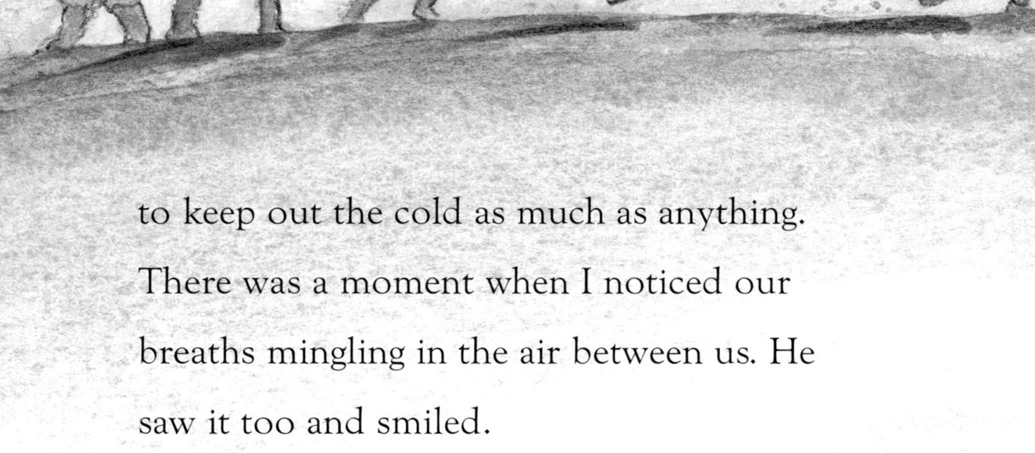

to keep out the cold as much as anything. There was a moment when I noticed our breaths mingling in the air between us. He saw it too and smiled.

"Jim Macpherson," he said after a while, "I think this is how we should resolve this war. A football match. No one dies in a football match. No children are orphaned.

No wives become widows."

"I'd prefer cricket," I told him. "Then we Tommies could be sure of winning, probably." We laughed at that, and together we watched the game. Sad to say, Connie, Fritz won, two goals to one. But as Hans Wolf generously said, our goal was wider than theirs, so it wasn't quite fair.

The time came, and all too soon, when the game was finished, the schnapps and the cake and the rum and the sausage had long since run out, and we knew it was all over. I wished Hans well and told him I hoped he would see his family again soon, that the fighting would end and we could all go home.

"I think that is what every soldier wants,

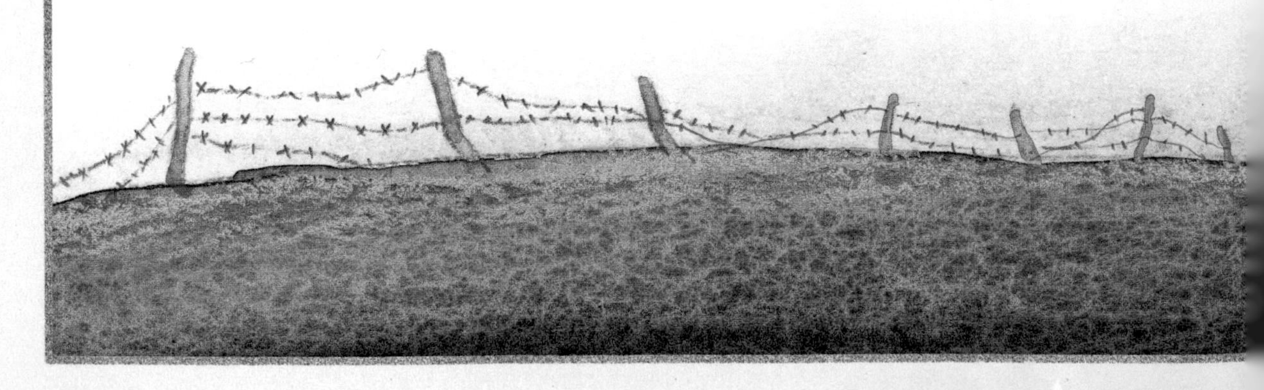

on both sides," Hans Wolf said. "Take care, Jim Macpherson. I shall never forget this moment, nor you."

He saluted and walked away from me slowly – unwillingly, I felt. He turned to wave just once and then became one of the hundreds of grey-coated men drifting back towards their trenches.

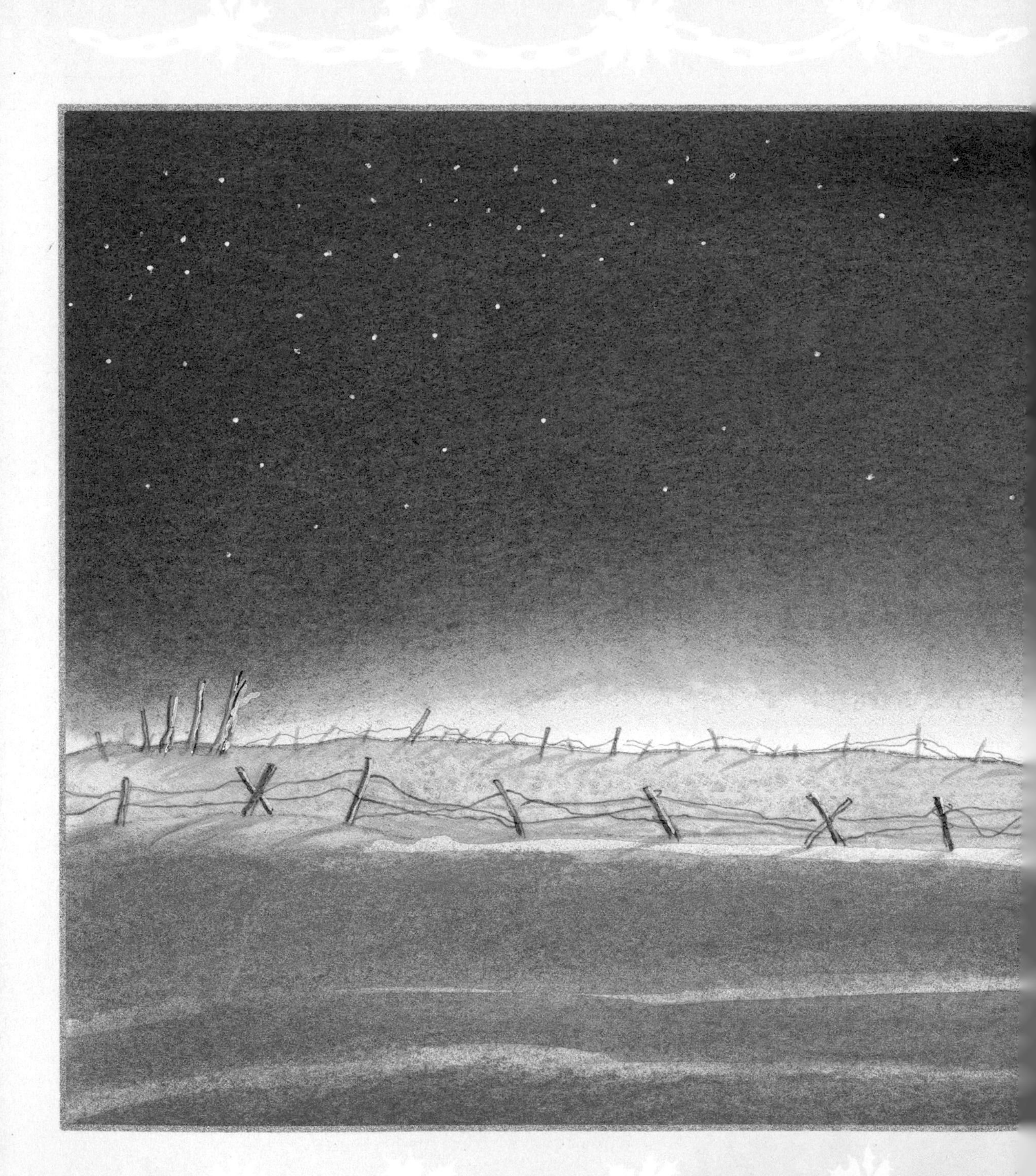

That night, back in our dugouts we heard them singing a carol, and singing it quite beautifully. It was ‘Stille Nacht’ – ‘Silent Night’. Our boys gave them a rousing chorus of ‘While shepherds watched’. We exchanged carols for a while and then we all fell silent. We had had our time of peace and goodwill, a time I will treasure as long as I live.

Dearest Connie, by Christmas time next year, this war will be nothing but a distant and terrible memory. I know from all that happened today how much both armies long for peace.
We shall be together again soon,
I'm sure of it.

Your loving Jim

I folded the letter again and slipped it carefully back into its envelope. I told no one about my find, but kept my shameful intrusion to myself. It was this guilt, I think, that kept me awake all night. By morning, I knew what I had to do. I made an excuse and did not go to church with the others. Instead I drove into Bridport, just a few miles away. I asked a boy walking his dog where Copper Beeches was.

Number twelve turned out to be nothing but a burnt-out shell, the roof gaping, the windows boarded up. I knocked at the house next door and asked if anyone knew the whereabouts of a Mrs Macpherson. Oh yes, said the old man in his slippers, he knew her well. A lovely old lady, he told me, a bit muddled-headed, but at her age she was entitled to be, wasn't she? 101 years old. She had been in the house when it caught fire. No one really knew how the fire had started, but it could well have been candles. She used candles rather than electricity, because she always thought electricity was too expensive. The fireman had got her out just in time. She was in a nursing home now, he told me, Burlington House, on the Dorchester road, on the other side of town.

I found Burlington House Nursing Home easily enough. There were paper chains up in the hallway and a lighted Christmas tree stood in the corner with a lop-sided angel on top. I said I was a friend come to visit Mrs Macpherson to bring her a Christmas present. I could see through into the dining room where everyone was wearing a paper hat

and singing along to 'Good King Wenceslas'. The matron had a hat on too and seemed happy enough to see me. She even offered me a mince pie. She walked me along the corridor.

"Mrs Macpherson is not in with the others," she told me. "She's rather confused today so we thought it best if she had a good rest. She's no family you know – no one visits. So I'm sure she'll be only too pleased to see you." She took me

into a conservatory with wicker chairs and potted plants all around and left me.

The old lady was sitting in a wheelchair, her hands folded in her lap. She had silver white hair pinned into a wispy bun. She was gazing out at the garden.

"Hello," I said.

She turned and looked up at me vacantly.

"Happy Christmas, Connie," I went on. "I found this. I think it's yours."

As I was speaking her eyes never left my face. I opened the tin box and gave it to her. That was the moment her eyes lit up with recognition and her face became suffused with a sudden glow of happiness. I explained about the desk, about how I had found it, but I don't think she was listening. For a while she said nothing, but stroked the letter tenderly with her fingertips.

Suddenly she reached out and took my

hand. Her eyes were filled with tears. “You told me you’d come home by Christmas, dearest,” she said. “And here you are, the best Christmas present in the world. Come closer, Jim dear, sit down.”

I sat down beside her, and she kissed my cheek. “I read your letter so often, Jim, every day. I wanted to hear your voice in my head. It always made me feel you were with me. And now you are. Now you’re

back you can read it to me yourself. Would you do that for me? I just want to hear your voice again, Jim. I'd love that so much. And then perhaps we'll have some tea. I've made you a nice Christmas cake, marzipan all around. I know how much you love marzipan."

For all the children who read this
on Christmas night.

M.M.

On Angel Wings

Illustrated by Quentin Blake

The truth is that once we weren't children any more we never did believe Grandpa's story, not really, much as we might have wanted to. It was just too improbable, too fantastical. We still loved listening to it, though. Christmas nights would never have been the same without it.

We'd be out there on the hillside, all of us together, keeping watch over the sheep by night. That's where he'd been on the first Christmas night all those years before, the night it happened – or that's what he told us. We'd be wrapped in our cloaks and huddled round the fire, the sheep shifting around us in the darkness, and we'd be ready and waiting for the story to begin. That's just how it was last night. Grandpa poked his shepherd's crook into the fire and sent a shower of sparks flying up into the night sky.

'When I was very little,' he began, 'I remember I used to think all the stars were made out of sparks like those, sparks that went on for ever, that never went out. Then one night, I'd have been nine, or maybe ten years old, something quite wonderful happened. Father and Uncle Zac were there, and my older brothers,

Reuben and Jacob. We were all tired and irritable. It had been a long, hard day. We'd lost a couple of lambs the night before, to a wolf maybe, or a jackal. So no one was singing around the fire that night. No one was even talking. I remember I was stabbing at the fire with my crook, making stars of the sparks, as I loved to do. Then it happened.

Instead of flying up high to join the stars, they seemed to be playing with one another, then arranging themselves into a figure, a human figure, that was bathed in sudden glorious light,

hovering over us, wings outstretched. It was an angel!

I threw myself into Father's arms and buried my face in his shoulder. When I dared look up again Uncle Zac and Reuben and Jacob were lying face down on the ground, Jacob sobbing like a baby. The sheep had scattered everywhere, bleating piteously.

"I'm sorry to drop in on you unexpectedly like this," said the angel. And at the sound of his voice the sheep fell silent around us. "It must be an awful shock. But believe me you've got nothing to worry about, nothing at all."

There was a comforting warmth to his voice, and a gentleness about him that was instantly reassuring. Uncle Zac and Reuben and Jacob were up on their knees by now, their faces filled not with fear, but with awe and wonder. The sheep were drifting back towards us, gazing up at the angel adoringly as if he were their shepherd. It was Uncle Zac who dared to speak first.

"Are you really an angel?" he breathed.

"I am," said the angel. "And my name is Gabriel."

"Are you really real?" Father asked, clutching me as tightly as I was clutching him. "Or are you a dream?"

"No dream," the Angel Gabriel replied. "What I am is real, and what I've come to tell you is true. I bring you news of great joy. For tonight, only a few miles away from here in Bethlehem a child has been born, a Saviour who is Christ the Lord. He will bring peace and goodwill to the whole world. Even as I speak, this child King, this son of God and son of man, is lying wrapped in swaddling clothes and cradled in a manger. I can see from your faces that you don't quite believe me, do you?"

"Kings are born in palaces," said Father.

"Not this King," replied the angel. "But seeing

is believing, isn't it? How would you like to go there? Would you like to see him for yourselves?"

"We'll go, of course we will," said Uncle Zac, getting to his feet. "But you'll have to tell us where to find him. There are dozens of stables in Bethlehem. How are we to know which one he is in?"

"It's simple," the Angel Gabriel said. "When I've gone you'll see a star in the eastern sky. Just follow it and it'll stop right over the stable. That's where you'll find the baby. What are you waiting for? Do you want to go, or don't you?"

"Why us?" asked Uncle Zac. "Why have you chosen us?"

"Because," replied the Angel Gabriel, "because one day he too will be a shepherd as you are, a shepherd not of sheep, but of all mankind."

"I don't like it," Reuben whispered to Uncle Zac. "How do we know it's true? It could be some sort of a trick, to get us to leave our sheep."

"Oh dear," sighed the Angel Gabriel. "I can see you're going to need some convincing."

As he spoke the sky above was suddenly filled with angels, hundreds of them, and the whole earth rang with their singing.

"Glory to God on high. And on earth, peace, goodwill towards men."

Even as they sang, they hovered above us, their wings beating the air so that there was a great rushing wind all about us that fanned the embers of the fire into sudden roaring flames.

Reuben and Jacob and Uncle Zac were flat on their faces again, but I watched. I watched all the time. I didn't want to miss a thing. I wasn't frightened at all, I was simply spellbound.

The angels were gone as unexpectedly as they had appeared, the Angel Gabriel too, leaving us alone with our sheep in the silence and the darkness of the hillside. It took a while for our eyes to become accustomed to the dark again. Father threw some more wood onto the fire, and when the sparks flew up I half expected them to become the Angel Gabriel again, but this time they just vanished into the blackness above.

"Look," Uncle Zac whispered. "Look up there in the east. That star! It's moving!"

And sure enough, there it was: a moving star low in the eastern sky, as bright a star as I'd ever seen.

"Come on. Let's follow it," Uncle Zac said. "We have to find out if this saviour has really come. We have to know if the child King is there."

"What about the sheep?" Father asked. "Who'll look after the sheep? We can't just leave them."

"Well, I'm not staying," said Reuben and Jacob in unison.

And suddenly everyone was looking at me and I could see at once the way it was going.

"Why me?" I protested. "What about the wolves? What about the jackals?"

"He's frightened of the dark," Jacob scoffed. "He's a scaredy cat."

"You've got the fire," Uncle Zac told me. "They won't come near the fire."

"We won't be gone long, son." Father might have sounded more sympathetic than my brothers, but he was still going with them. They were still leaving me alone. "Bethlehem's just over the hill. We'll be back before dawn."

"But we could take the sheep with us," I pleaded. "Then we could all go."

"You can't move sheep in the dark, stupid," Reuben said.

"But why me?" I cried. "It's just because I'm the youngest. It's not fair." No one was listening to me.

"Don't worry," said Father, trying to console me as they made ready to go. "We'll tell you all about the baby when we get back. Promise. You just keep the fire going and look after the sheep. You'll be quite safe."

And off they went, shadows drifting away into the night, leaving me. I had never felt so alone, nor so miserable as I did then. Sitting by the fire, pulling my cloak around me, I cursed my luck for being the youngest, and my father for abandoning me, and began to sob my heart out. Lifting my head I let out a huge wail of anger and despair that echoed over the hills.

"It's not fair! It's not fair!"

As the echoes died I became suddenly aware that I was not alone any more. There, opposite me in the glowing light of the fire, sat the Angel Gabriel.

"You don't sound very happy," he said. "They left you behind, didn't they? Well someone had to look after the sheep, I suppose."

"I suppose," I said, so relieved not to be alone any more.

"You're right though," said the Angel Gabriel, "about life not being fair. So I've had this idea, to make it a little fairer. I could fly you there to the stable. We could be there and back, lickety-split, and no one would ever know you'd been gone."

"You could fly me there?" I cried, more excited than I had been in all my life. "You could really do that?"

"Easy as pie," he said.

At that moment a sheep and her lamb came and lay down beside me, as if to remind me of my duty. I knew I couldn't leave them.

"The sheep," I said, suddenly downcast. "There'd be no one to look after the sheep."

"Have you forgotten my heavenly chorus?" said the Angel Gabriel. "They don't just sing, you know."

And even as he spoke the sky above us burst into light and out of the light they came floating down – who knows how many? – landing softly on their feet in amongst the sheep who seemed not in the least alarmed.

"Enough to do the job, I think, don't you?" laughed the Angel Gabriel. "Now, hop on. We haven't a moment to lose."

I did as he told me. Still clutching my shepherd's crook, I vaulted onto his back and clung on. So I left the sheep with their guardian angels and lifted off, my arms around the Angel Gabriel's neck.

"Hang on," he said laughing, "but don't throttle me, there's a good lad."

And so we rose into the sky, leaving the sheep below with the guardian angels now as their shepherds.

On we flew along black glassy rivers, up and down hills, his great wings beating strongly, slowly. And always we went eastwards, the star ahead of us, beckoning us on. I wanted it to go on for ever and ever, even though the cold numbed my fingers, numbed my face, and made my eyes water. I saw the lights of the little town flickering beneath us. We saw where the star had stopped, saw the lights of the stable below. We floated gently to earth in the courtyard of an inn.

The town lay asleep all around us, still and silent, except for a couple of dogs that barked at one another. Cats slunk everywhere into dark alleyways, their eyes glinting.

"You go in alone," said the Angel Gabriel. "His mother is called Mary, his father is Joseph. Off you go now."

The guttering glow of yellow lamplight seemed to be inviting me in. The door was half open. I stepped in.

It was much like any other stable I'd been in – warm and dusty and smelly. A couple of donkeys were lying side by side, their great ears following me, their eyes watching me with dreamy indifference. In the dim light of the stable I could see several oxen chewing their cud, grunting contentedly.

One of them licked deep into her nose as I passed by. I could still see no baby, no Christ child, no King. I was beginning to wonder if the angel had brought me to the wrong place. Then from a stall at the far end of the stable came a man's voice.

"We're over here," he said. "Where the sheep are. Careful you don't tread on them."

The sheep shifted as I walked slowly through them. A lamb came skittering out of the shadows and suckled his mother furiously, his tail waggling with wild delight.

It was then I saw them, at last, their faces bright in the lamplight.

"Come closer," said Mary. "You won't be disturbing him. He's wide awake."

She was sitting propped up in the hay, the baby cradled in her arms. All I could see of him was a pink face and one tiny hand which he waved a little and then promptly shoved in his mouth. He was looking at me, straight at me, and when at last he took his fist out of his mouth, he smiled, and it was a smile I have never forgotten, a smile of such love that it moves my heart to this day whenever I think of it.

I crouched down in the straw

beside them and when I offered him my finger, he clung onto it and didn't seem to want to let go.

"He's strong," I said.

"He'll need to be," said Joseph.

We talked in whispers, the three of us, and Joseph told me how ashamed he was not to have found a better place for Mary to give birth, but that everywhere in Bethlehem, all the inns, were full.

"It's fine," said Mary. "It's warm in here and his manger's full of soft hay for a cradle. He has all he needs, and now he has his first visitor. Would you like to hold him for a while?"

I had never in all my life held a baby before – plenty of lambs, but never a baby. Joseph showed me how to do it. Babies were easier, I discovered. They didn't wriggle so much.

"What's he called?" I asked, cradling him in my arms, hoping against hope he wouldn't cry.

"Jesus," Mary said. "We're calling him Jesus."

So for a few precious minutes I held him in my arms, the child that has been the light of my life ever since.

I stayed until they laid him in his manger of hay, until he fell asleep, and Mary too. Then Joseph took me back through the sheep to the stable door to say goodbye.

"There may be more visitors tonight," said Joseph. "But you were the first. We shan't forget you."

"Nor I you," I replied. It was only then, as I was about to go, that it occurred to me I had forgotten something.

"Whenever a child is born in our village," I said, "everyone brings a present. This is all I've got with me." And I handed Joseph my shepherd's crook. "Father made it for me. He said it should last a lifetime."

"Thank you," Joseph said, running his hand along the crook. "This is wonderful work, the work of a craftsman. He will have no finer gift than this." And with that he turned and went back inside.

Moments later the Angel Gabriel was winging me away, out over the walls of the stable yard, over the sleeping town, away from the light of the star and back towards the darkness of the hills.

As we flew I was full of questions. I wanted to know so much about Jesus, this child King who was going to save the world.

"How will he do it?" I shouted into Gabriel's ear against the sound of the wind. "How will he bring us peace and goodwill?"

The Angel Gabriel flew on, never answering any of my questions. It was almost as if he hadn't heard me at all. Only when we landed in amongst the sheep and the shepherd angels did he at last give me an answer.

"Love," he said. "He will bring us love, and through love we will at last have peace and goodwill on earth. Now, make sure you keep the fire going, there's a good lad."

Those were the last words he spoke to me. There were no goodbyes. There was no time. He rose at once into the night sky, and with him all the other angels too, each a beacon of sparkling light. And as they went I heard first the singing of their wings, then the singing of their voices until the sky above me and the whole earth rang with such a joyful sound that I thought my heart would burst.

"Glory to God on high. And on earth, peace, goodwill towards men."

Slowly the music faded and the light died. I felt suddenly alone in the night until the sheep gathered

about me, all of us, I know, sharing the wonder of everything we had just witnessed.

Father and the others came back just after sunrise, full of everything, of course, and very pleased with themselves. They'd followed the star and found the stable and the child King wrapped in swaddling clothes. He'd been fast asleep in his manger, they said, all the time they were there.

"Such a pity you couldn't have been with us," Reuben sniggered.

"Then these three Kings from far off Persian lands turned up, and there wasn't room for us

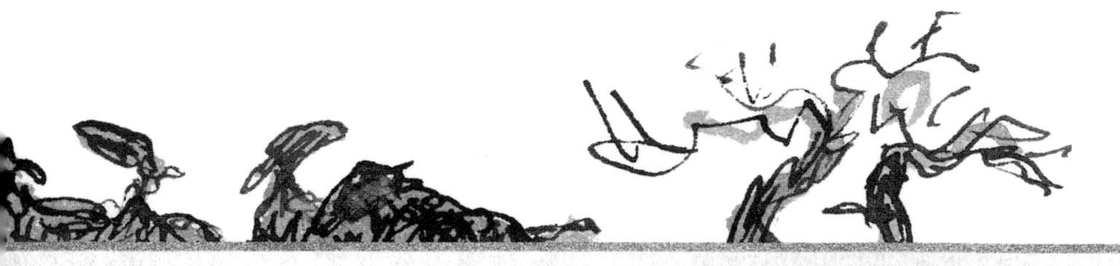

and we had to go," said Uncle Zac, who sounded more than a little put out. "You should've seen the presents they brought: gold, frankincense, myrrh. We had nothing to give him except our crooks and we couldn't hardly give him those, could we?"

"Proper stupid we felt," Jacob added.

"Sheep all right?" Father asked me. "Anything happen while we were gone?"

"Not a thing," I replied. "Not a thing."

I nearly told them then, so nearly. I was bursting to tell them everything. But I didn't, because I knew they'd never have believed me anyway. Reuben and Jacob would only have scoffed and laughed at me even more than usual. Just keep quiet about it, I told myself. When the time comes you can tell your children and your grandchildren, because they'll know about Jesus by then – everyone will. And you do too, don't you, his whole life, everything he did and said. You may not believe my story but you don't laugh at me, you don't scoff. You just think I'm a bit old, a bit doolally. And I suppose I am at that.'

And Grandpa always ended his story the same way, his voice almost a whisper. 'And that shepherd's crook I gave him – I told Father I'd lost it in the dark that night and he made me another – Jesus carried it with him all his life. It was there at the Sermon on the Mount; when he fed the five thousand; when he rode into Jerusalem. He had it with him almost to the end, till they took it off him, till that last day when he carried the cross instead.'

And so Grandpa finished his story. But that wasn't the end of it, not last night. Last night the story had a very different ending altogether, something amazing, incredible – which is why I've written it down at once. This way I'll always be able to remember it as it was and I'll never be able to believe it didn't happen.

As we sat there around the fire, silent in our thoughts, I thought, as all of us did, that Grandpa's Christmas story was over for another year. It was such a lovely story, but just a story. We knew how Grandpa had followed Jesus all his life, how much he loved him. Wishful thinking, we thought, that's all it had been, just wishful thinking. But I remember sitting there last night and wondering whether any of it could possibly be true. That was when it happened.

Grandpa began prodding at the fire with his shepherd's crook. Showers of sparks rose into the night sky and as I watched them I saw that they did not fly up towards the stars, but gathered themselves into a great light. And within the light I saw beacons of brightness that took shape and became angels, hundreds of them, thousands of them, their wings singing in the air, then their voices too, until the skies above us rang with such joyful sounds that I thought my heart would burst.

'Glory to God on high!' they sang. 'And on earth, peace, goodwill towards men!'

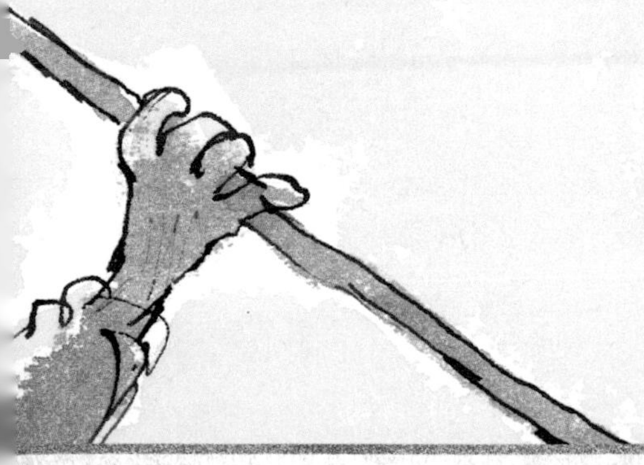

For Isla and Alara,
their story.

M.M.

Mimi and the Mountain Dragon

Illustrated by Helen Stephens

Every Christmas Eve in the little village of Dorta where I grew up, high in the mountains of Switzerland, we have a carnival, a carnival like no other. We call it "Drumming the Mountain Dragon".

Everyone gathers around the Great Bear, the statue that stands in the middle of the village square. Sounding our hunting horns, and banging our drums, and not only drums but pots and pans too, we make our way up through the streets.

The children lead the way, cracking their long whips and yelling as loud as they can. Even the smallest children join in.

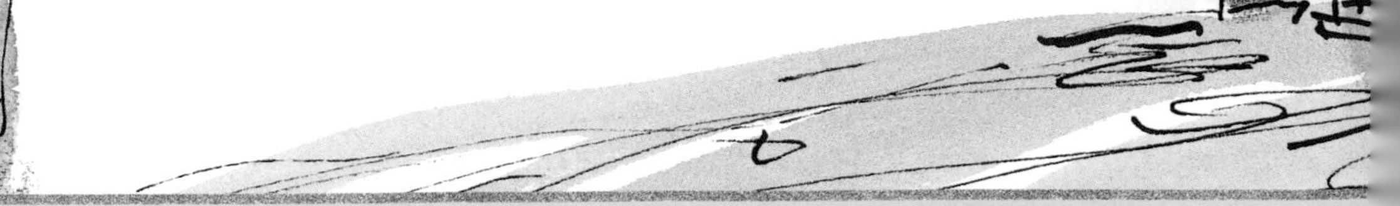

Wrapped up on their sleds, they blow whistles, shake rattles, or bang away on their tambourines.

We troop through the village until we're out on the snow-covered slopes right under the mountain, all of us banging and clanging, shouting our defiance, letting that beastly Mountain Dragon know just how we feel, telling her to stay in her castle and leave us in peace for another year.

Then the next evening, and of course it's Christmas Day by now, all of us gather in the village square again, not with hunting horns and drums and whips, but with bells, sheep bells for little children, and cow bells for everyone else.

We carry flaming torches partly to light the way, partly to keep us warm. We go the same way we went the day before, but this time ringing our bells. We climb up higher than we did on Christmas Eve, right up to the tree line below the castle walls. Here we always stop and listen to the mountains above, echoing with the sound of our bells. Then we sing a Christmas carol, to the Mountain Dragon, and always the same carol: "Sweet bells, sweet chiming Christmas bells".

Now, after the last echoes have died away, comes the time for the story, the story of Mimi and the Mountain Dragon, *the story that reminds us each year why we have our carnival on Christmas Eve, why we come back up the mountainside again on Christmas Day, and why this time we come ringing our bells and singing our carols.*

The storyteller is chosen by lottery, a name plucked from a hat. This last Christmas time it was my name that came out. I was the storyteller. Everyone hurled their flaming torches into a heap to make a bonfire, and we clustered round it.

"Don't make it too long, Michael," the Mayor told me, "or, bonfire or not, we'll freeze to death up here. Always remember the story has to warm our hearts and warm our toes at the same time."

Keeping his advice in mind, I began my telling of the story.

Mimi and the Mountain Dragon

"This story happened a long, long time ago, before the first cars and tourists and skiers ever came to our little village. No one came here, except passing tradesmen, or the occasional traveller lost in a blizzard and seeking shelter for a night.

In winter-time, snow would cut the village off from the rest of the world for months on end. Families and their animals huddled together under the same roof, to keep warm, to survive. And in summer-time, every daylight hour was spent growing and harvesting corn and hay and straw, gathering berries and herbs and mushrooms from the mountainsides, fattening the pigs and sheep, making cheese, and bringing in enough firewood from the forests.

By Christmas each year they were in the depths of winter, and everyone was longing for the dark nights to shorten, for the snows to melt away in spring, for sunshine to light up the world. But Christmas for the villagers then wasn't simply to celebrate the promise of spring to come, or even the birth of a baby in Bethlehem 2,000 years before.

All the singing of carols, the ringing of bells, the merrymaking, the dancing and the feasting, had another purpose too: to drive away the evil spirits they knew were lurking in the darkness outside. And there was one evil spirit above all that frightened and threatened them: the Mountain Dragon.

This terrible dragon lived in the castle ruins high above the village. No one had ever set eyes on her, but everyone knew she was up there, because when she became angry she would rage and roar in her castle lair, and bring death and disaster down upon our village below. She would spew out fire, setting the forests ablaze in summer. And in winter she would shake the mountain with lightning and thunder, so that the snow would break loose and slide down the mountainside in huge avalanches. Many houses and many people had vanished under these avalanches, never to be seen again. And if anyone disappeared in the mountains, a child playing by a stream, a hunter out in the forest, a villager gathering berries, it was the Mountain Dragon who had carried them off to her lair in the castle.

The villagers tried everything to protect themselves from this merciless dragon. They prayed in church, they laid curses on her, they burnt effigies of her. And every year on Christmas Eve they would gather in the village square and set out for the Mountain Dragon's castle, banging their drums, blowing their hunting horns, cracking their whips. 'Do your worst!' they'd cry, when they came as close to

the castle as they dared.
'We're not frightened of you!
You huff and you puff all you like!
We don't care! We're staying! This
is our mountain, our village, not yours!'

Then they'd set up a chanting that echoed
all round the mountains and down the valley.
'Death to the Mountain Dragon! Death
to the Mountain Dragon!'

And this was how it went on
every Christmas Eve for
hundreds of years.

Then early one Christmas Day, the morning after the Drumming the Mountain Dragon carnival, something amazing happened, something so extraordinary that it changed the fortunes of the village, of all of us, for ever.

They say it all began in the year of 1314. Mimi Arquint was the only child of a farming family living in a house below the little chapel of San Bastian. That snowy Christmas morning, Mimi went out across the yard to the woodshed to fetch in the logs, as she always did. She was still only half awake as she opened the door. So it took a while after the brightness of the snow for her eyes to become accustomed to the dark of the shed.

At first she could not believe what she thought she was seeing. Rubbing her eyes and blinking hard didn't make it go away. Mimi thought it might be some kind of vision left over from some half-forgotten dream. But the moments passed and the vision was still there.

There could be no doubt about it, her eyes were not playing tricks on her. It was lying there curled up on the woodpile. A baby dragon! He was entirely green from head to tail. His eyes were closed, and he was snoring softly, a strangely soothing sound, almost as if he was humming his own lullaby. Little puffs of smoke rose into the air in time with the baby dragon's musical snoring. It was a lovely tune, a simple tune, so Mimi found herself almost at once able to hum along in perfect harmony. As she hummed, she felt so overwhelmed with tenderness for him,

so sure he would not harm her, that she reached out and touched his neck with her fingertips. At this the little dragon opened his eyes, which were as green as the rest of him, and looked up at her, not in fear, but in wonder.

'I'll look after you, I promise,' she whispered.

That was when there came a sudden loud bellowing from across the yard. It was her father.

'Where's that firewood, Mimi?' he shouted crossly. 'The oven's going out! Do I have to come and fetch it myself?'

'I'm coming, Papi!' she called out. Mimi knew well enough what Papi would do if he discovered there was a baby dragon in the woodshed.

'Death to the Mountain Dragon! Death to the Mountain Dragon!' Hadn't the whole village, Papi along with them, chanted that together only the day before? She had to hurry. But to her astonishment, when she turned round again, the dragon was nowhere to be seen. Maybe she had been imagining him after all.

But a few moments later she heard the sound of his humming from above her head. There he was, perched high on a rafter, wings outstretched in alarm, wide-eyed and breathing hard. She could see at once how frightened he was.

'It's all right,' said Mimi. 'Come back down. I won't hurt you. I won't let anyone hurt you.' She held out her arm. 'Come on, little dragon.' Mimi knew he would come when he was ready. And so he did, floating down on outstretched wings and landing on her wrist. His claws may have been long and sharp, but he did not hurt her. As he sat there she sang softly to him, her favourite Christmas carol, 'Sweet bells, sweet chiming Christmas Bells'. And now when he hummed, it was her tune he seemed to be humming. It was his way of speaking to her, telling her he trusted her. Music was the language of dragons!

'I don't think anyone knows dragons like music,' Mimi said. 'Does your mother sing to you, like Mutti sings to me? And your mother, she's up there in her castle, isn't she, worried sick about you? And you've gone off and got yourself lost, haven't you?'

'Breakfast, Mimi!' came Mutti's voice now from across the yard. 'Hurry up, or we'll be late for church!'

'And bring that wood!' Papi was yelling.

'Coming, Papi! Coming, Mutti!' Mimi cried.

'I've got to go,' she told the little dragon, stroking his neck with the back of her finger. 'You must be starving, you poor thing. I'll fetch you some breakfast, shall I? Do dragons eat honey cake? I bet they do. I'll get you some. And afterwards, I'd better get you back home before your mother comes looking. She's the Mountain Dragon, isn't she? And she's going to be so angry if she discovers where you are. She'll think we've stolen you away or something.

She'll be furious, and if the Mountain Dragon gets angry, if she starts roaring and raging, well . . . anything could happen.'

Mimi settled him back on the woodpile, and quickly gathered up some logs. 'I'll be back soon with your breakfast,' she told the little dragon. And off she went with her logs, leaving him in the dark of the woodshed.

As usual there was honey cake and hot milk for breakfast. Mimi drank the milk but didn't eat the honey cake. She had plans for it. Mimi longed to tell Mutti all about the little dragon in the woodshed, but Papi was always there in the kitchen with them; and Papi wasn't just a farmer, he was a hunter, and a good one too. There was the bearskin on the chair

to remind her, and antlers on the walls everywhere.

'You're very quiet this morning, Mimi,' said Mutti. 'It's Christmas Day. You should be happy. And you haven't touched your honey cake. Are you all right, dear?'

'I'm fine, Mutti,' Mimi told her. 'I just don't feel like eating, that's all.'

'Wasn't it the best yesterday?' said Papi, tucking into his honey cake. 'Wasn't that the best carnival ever? We showed that nasty old dragon, didn't we, Mimi? She'll hide away in her castle all year after that. No forest fires this year, no avalanches.'

'We'll see.' Mutti didn't sound so sure. 'Every Christmas Eve we go out drumming the Mountain Dragon, but every year we still have a fire, don't we? Or an avalanche? Or someone goes up onto the mountain and doesn't come back? If you ask me, all that drumming may make us feel better, but it doesn't seem to do much good.'

At that moment the church bells began to ring. Mutti got up in a hurry and cleared away the table. Papi was putting on his coat. So neither of them noticed Mimi squirrelling away

her piece of honey cake in her pocket. Then she was out of the door before they could stop her. 'I'll meet you in church,' she cried. 'There's something I have to do first. Byee!'

'Where are you going, Mimi?' Mutti called after her. But she was gone.

As she ran across the farmyard, she could see the villagers tramping their way to church through the snow, their breath smokey on the air – just like my little dragon, Mimi thought. Close to the woodshed now, she began to hum 'Sweet bells' to let the little dragon know it was she who was coming, so he wouldn't be frightened.

She found him waiting for her on the woodpile exactly where she had left him, still snoring, smokily, still humming. Mimi crouched down and fed him the honey cake. He finished every last crumb of it, licking his lips again and again, in case there was a crumb he had missed. That was when Mimi caught sight of his teeth for the very first time, and was suddenly just a little afraid. They looked as sharp as icicles, and there were so many of them. But his eyes were smiling up at her and she knew there was nothing to be afraid of.

'I've worked it all out,' Mimi said. 'As soon as the bells stop ringing, we'll know that everyone is safely inside the church. On Christmas Day everyone goes to church, even Papi, so no one will be about, no one will see us. Do you know what I'm going to do? I'm going to carry you home to your mother, back up to the Mountain Dragon's castle. That's where you live, isn't it?'

All the while as she was speaking, the little dragon had his head on one side, listening to every word. 'Your mother, she won't hurt me, will she? She won't blast me with her fire?'

He began humming again then, but louder, more urgently. The louder he hummed, the deeper the breaths he took, and the more he puffed out his smoke. He wafted his tail to and fro. Mimi was sure he was trying to tell her something,

And then she understood what it had to be. Everything would be fine if she hummed, if she sang. That's what made the little dragon happy, so that's what would make the Mountain Dragon happy too. Music!

The church bells stopped ringing. It was time to go, and the little dragon seemed to know it. He spread his wings, lifted off the woodpile and landed gently on Mimi's shoulder. Out they went together into the farmyard. The cows were in the snow-covered meadow. The sound of their ding-donging bells filled the air all around, as Mimi walked through the herd. Martha, always the friendliest of the cows, came wandering over to her to be stroked. But once she saw the little dragon, she stopped, looking sideways at her, and snorting.

'It's all right, Martha,' Mimi said, 'he's a dragon,

but he's only a baby dragon. He won't hurt you.' That was when the idea came to her. 'Martha, can I borrow your bell? I'll bring it back, I promise.' And Mimi reached out and unfastened the bell from around Martha's neck. She didn't seem to mind at the time, but afterwards she did follow them for a while through the snow, mooing mournfully as Mimi walked away up the mountain, the little dragon on her shoulder, ringing the cow bell and humming as she went.

'Sweet bells, sweet chiming Christmas bells', Mimi was singing out loud now, the little dragon humming along in her ear. It was a steep climb, and steeper still the closer they came to the trees and the castle beyond.

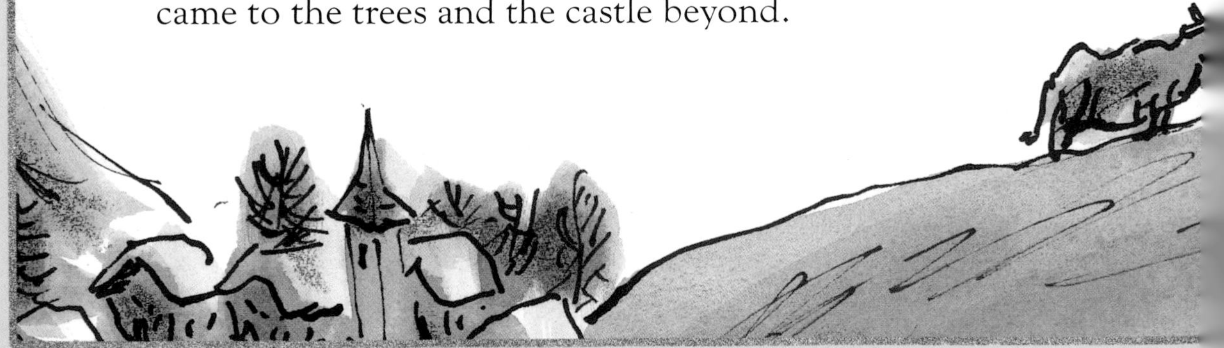

She was finding it harder and harder to keep going, and to keep singing, and it wasn't only because she was tired. Every time she glanced up at the looming grey walls of the castle, her heart filled with fear.

There was a moment when she thought she couldn't go on. She was standing in deep snow, looking back down at the village, at the church steeple, knowing that Mutti and Papi and everyone else was there.

She longed to be safe inside the church with them. She could just hear them singing 'Sweet bells, sweet chiming Christmas bells'. That sound was all she needed to lift her spirits, to give her the courage she needed to go on.

On she tramped through the snow, ringing her bell, singing out as loud as she could, the little dragon still humming in her ear. Onwards and upwards, onwards and upwards, until she found herself at last right under the castle walls, with only the drawbridge between her and the great wooden doors of the castle.

'What do I do now, little dragon?'

Mimi whispered. 'Is this where you live? Is this where the Mountain Dragon really lives?'

At that very moment, she saw the castle doors yawning open, and there at the far end of the drawbridge stood the Mountain Dragon herself, more monstrous, more terrifying than Mimi had ever imagined she could be. She stood as high as the church steeple, green and scaly from head to tail, just like the little dragon, but her brow was heavy with anger and her eyes blazed with fury. Fiery smoke billowed from her nostrils, and she pawed the ground with her great claws like a bull ready to charge.

All Mimi wanted to do was to turn and run, but her legs would not move. She was rooted to the spot with terror. Any moment now, she could be torn to pieces by those terrible claws, or burnt to cinders by a single blast of the Mountain Dragon's fiery breath.

But suddenly, the little dragon began to cheep and flap his wings excitedly, and with a screech of joy, he took off. He wasn't that clever at flying yet, so he didn't quite manage to make it all the way across the drawbridge.

He landed clumsily, tumbling over and over, and then stumbling on through the snow till he ended up at his mother's feet.

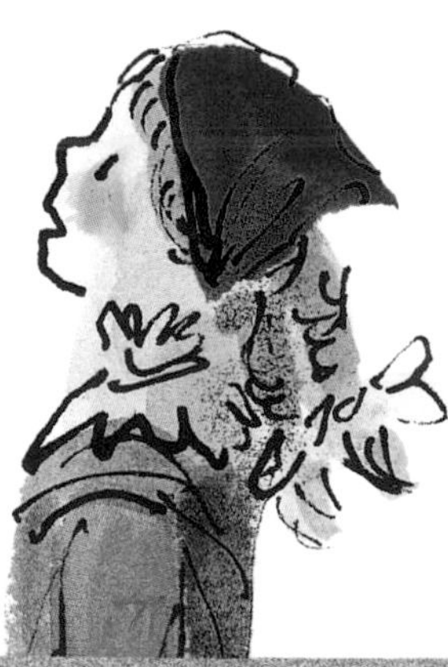

The Mountain Dragon looked down lovingly at him, then bent to gather him up. Gently she held him, sweetly she hummed to him. And Mimi could hear him humming back.

But now, the reunion over, the Mountain Dragon turned her attention to Mimi once more, and began walking slowly across the drawbridge towards her. Closer came those claws, closer came that scaly monstrous head, that fiery breath, so close now that Mimi could feel the heat of it. She did not

back away, though. She felt no need to, because there was no anger in the Mountain Dragon's eyes any more, only kindness and tenderness.

Slowly the Mountain Dragon lowered her head, near enough now for Mimi to reach out her hand to touch her nose. And this she did, because she knew that she had nothing to fear, that this terrifying creature could be kind and tender, like any mother, like Mutti.

Why it should have happened that the mountain above the castle began at that particular moment to shed itself of its winter snows, none will ever know. But it did. And as Mimi could clearly see, it was not the Mountain Dragon roaring and raging that set the avalanche tumbling and rumbling down the mountainside. Mimi had no time even to be frightened, for, along with the little dragon, she was suddenly whisked up into the air, and onto the Mountain Dragon's shoulders.

There, side by side, they both clung on for dear life, as the Mountain

Dragon spread her wings, and lifting off, flew up and away, high above the castle, high above the mountain peaks. Mimi could only look down in horror as the avalanche gathered speed, thundering down towards the village, towards the church, tearing rocks and trees out of the ground as it went, covering houses and barns, filling the streets and the village square, snapping the church steeple in two like a matchstick, and smothering entirely the church beneath.

All was still now, all was silent. The avalanche was over. The village and everyone who lived there were buried underneath the snow.

Mimi was yelling in the Mountain Dragon's ear now: 'Mutti's in the church, Papi too! Everyone is in there!'

The Mountain Dragon flew down, circling the village once, and landing beside the broken church steeple. She drew herself up to her full height, took a deep breath, and blasted out her fire. At once the snow began to melt away. Again and again she did it, until the roof and the walls of the church could be seen, and the windows, and the

doorway, until the first of the villagers emerged from inside, utterly bewildered and astonished. Imagine Mimi's great joy and relief when she saw Mutti and Papi coming out too.

And what did they see? The Mountain Dragon walking through the village, breathing out her fire, melting the snow all around her; and Mimi and the little dragon were riding on her shoulders. Within an hour or so, every house and every barn was clear of snow, and the streets ran like rushing torrents. Not a single soul died that day in Dorta, not a horse, not a cow (not Martha!), not a sheep, not a pig, not even a hen.

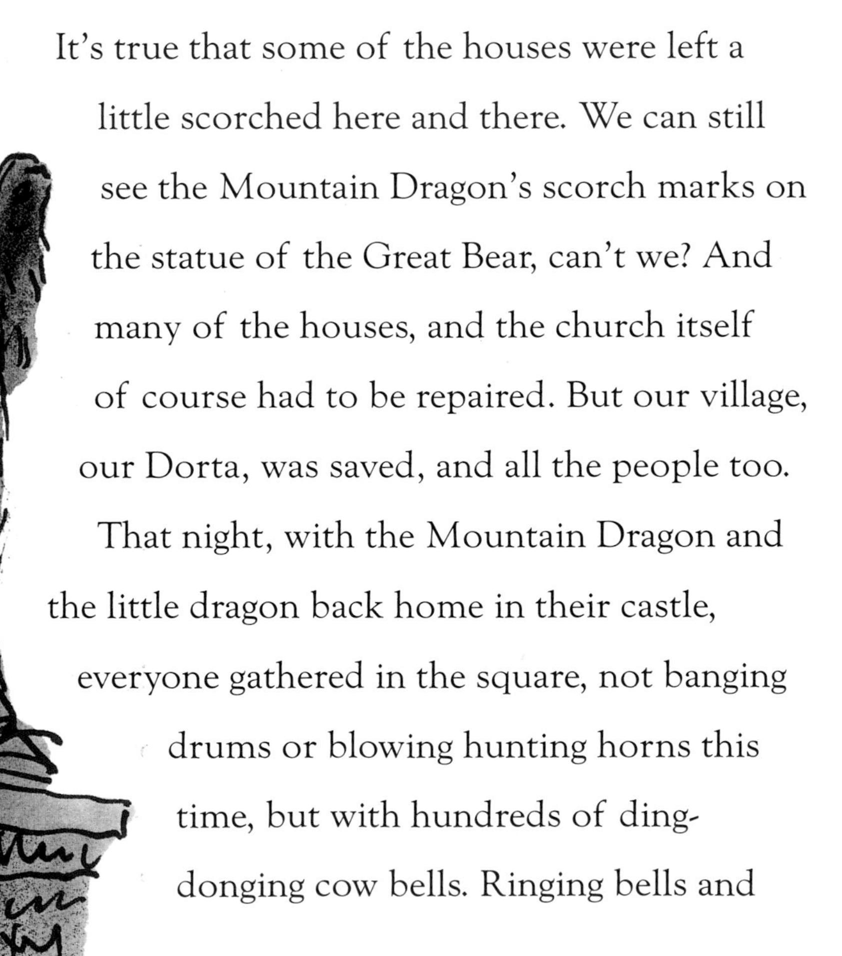

It's true that some of the houses were left a little scorched here and there. We can still see the Mountain Dragon's scorch marks on the statue of the Great Bear, can't we? And many of the houses, and the church itself of course had to be repaired. But our village, our Dorta, was saved, and all the people too.

That night, with the Mountain Dragon and the little dragon back home in their castle, everyone gathered in the square, not banging drums or blowing hunting horns this time, but with hundreds of ding-donging cow bells. Ringing bells and carrying flaming torches, they made their way up to the castle. And here, right where we're standing tonight, under the castle walls, they sang Mimi's favourite carol, 'Sweet bells, sweet chiming Christmas bells'.

And from that day to this, with the Mountain Dragon, and the little dragon, looking out for us and protecting us, we have never once had an avalanche anywhere near the village, nor a forest fire, and no one ever since has disappeared in the mountains.

But what does it mean, this little story of ours that we know so well? I think it means many things: that dragons need not be the dragons we believe them to be; that little children, like Mimi, sometimes know better than grown-up children; and that sweet bells, sweet chiming bells can bring us all new hope and joy and peace at Christmas time."

As usual after the story – whoever had done the telling – everyone clapped and cheered, and clanged their bells.

The Mayor clapped me on the back and told me I'd told it well. "It could have been a little shorter, Michael," he said. "But bravo all the same."

With the bonfire of torches almost burnt out by now, we all wanted to get back to the warmth of our homes. I stayed behind for just a while longer, as I often had done as a little boy, hoping that just this once, I might catch a glimpse of the Mountain Dragon high on the ramparts, and maybe the little dragon too. They didn't show themselves. They never have done.

But they are up there, I know they are.

EGMONT

We bring stories to life

Christmas Stories first published in Great Britain 2012 by Egmont UK Limited
Published in this edition, with *Mimi and the Mountain Dragon* added, in Great Britain 2015
by Egmont UK Limited, The Yellow Building, 1 Nicholas Road, London W11 4AN

ISBN 978 1 4052 6911 7

www.egmont.co.uk

A CIP catalogue record for this title is available from the British Library.